Th[...]

by [Michael McCloskey]

ISBN: 978-1481100007

Cover art by Howard Lyon

For my family.

Special thanks to Maarten Hofman and
Howard Lyon.

Prologue

Jack DeVries scanned the alien landscape from the overhang that concealed his tiny starship. Chigran Callnir Four looked like a combination of a rocky highland and a jungle. He saw heavy vegetation, or at least things that resembled trees and plants, though they apparently didn't shed leaves or branches since they grew out of gaps in the naked red rocks nearby with no sign of detritus.

DeVries didn't know anything about the planet except that it was one of the open worlds, meaning it could have picked up a settlement or two, provided there wasn't some deadly menace hiding among the rocks. DeVries didn't care much one way or the other. He just had to hang low for a few Earth Standard Months until the space force gave up searching for him. And whatever might be out there, he figured he was probably deadlier.

The last operation had been a messy one. He'd gotten away with the AI core just as planned. The only snag had been that he'd had to kill fifty-seven citizens to do it. Eight of them with his bare hands. DeVries did not look particularly strong or threatening, but that just added to his effectiveness.

DeVries slipped a water sensor out of his Veer skinsuit and gave the horizon a quick go over. He frowned. Nothing special out there, but at least he detected a large water source within three kilometers. There was also a speckling of water on the readings in his PV, which could be smaller pools or creatures largely composed of water. From his experience, they looked like Terran-sized collections of water, but he could not be sure.

He pocketed the scanner and made his way down the rocky hillside. A homogenous batch of plants dotted the way. Each had a thick trunk emerging from the rocks, which split into three branches, then each of those split again into three more until finally sprouting out into a flower or complex leaf that looked like a patch of green hair.

The plentiful plant stalks eased his descent, providing him with dozens of ready handles to steady him as he scrambled down the sharp rocks. Each of the stalks originated from a deep fissure in the rock along with ten or twenty others. If he did fall, he felt his suit would protect him as long as he didn't smash his head.

I wonder if the lack of accumulated leaves or branches on the ground is because something eats it all. But then I'd expect to see a bed of dung.

He peered into a hole where many stalks emerged. It was too dark to see inside.

Maybe the rain washes everything down these holes. Oh well. What do I care?

A red ribbon wrapped around a plant just ahead caught his attention. The strip of color shifted. DeVries struggled to resolve the image. The creature was half red and half diaphanous, resembling a snake or eel. Its translucent parts made it hard to see as it shifted position, fooling the eyes. It was much larger than it first appeared. DeVries was instantly wary.

He pulled out a light plastic dagger and altered course.

No point in messing with it unless it's coming after me.

The creature flowed to the top of its plant, then rose up even higher. Its upper body waved half a meter into the air as DeVries sidetracked it. He couldn't see any eyes or a mouth, but obviously it had detected his approach.

Danger display? Or is it just curious?

He could not help but compare it to similar creatures he knew about: large snakes and eels. He thought of constriction and poison. He considered drawing the stunner, but instead he simply kept moving steadily, climbing to one side. DeVries knew he had at least one thing going for him: whatever that thing's natural prey was, chances were he did not match its appearance or behavior.

That meant the feeding action of the animal most likely would not trigger on him.

Unless that thing just eats everything that moves.

The tense moment passed as he put several stalks between himself and the creature. It relaxed back into its previous pose, wrapped lazily around a plant or two. DeVries left the thing behind as he slipped the rest of the way down from the formation that concealed his ship. Then the ground angled back up again, toward the side of the next long, rocky hill. A line of vegetation limited his view down toward the valley he had examined from above. The water source was higher, between two hills.

He walked up the draw, remaining wary. He hopped from rock to rock trying to avoid the plants and thus hopefully the fauna as well. A cliff rose on his right, starting as a small cleft in the rock then rising meter after meter until it was a sheer rocky barrier.

DeVries found a cave entrance in the side of the cliff. When he stopped to examine it, he quickly noticed the entrance had been carved smooth. A ceramic grating of an odd design blocked the way. The grating had about a dozen strong vertical bars, with about eight centimeters of space between each one. The bars were only about four centimeters wide, but very deep. The openings extended about thirty centimeters to the far side. He resisted the urge to try and stick his arm through one. The other side was dark, and he didn't feel like finding out what danger might lurk there.

DeVries grunted. Apparently, the water wasn't his alone.

Unless whoever made this is long fallen to dust. Could be a ruin.

He accessed his scanner over his link. Without taking the device out of his pack, the scanner had a limited range, but DeVries just wanted to check for nearby danger. The scanner picked up some anomalies ahead. DeVries carefully cleared a rise of spiky rock and tried again.

Lifeforms. Humans. Now he was sure.

Can't be the space force. This has to be colonists. Out here in the middle of nowhere? Oh, of course. They must be here for the water, same as me.

DeVries took stock of his gear. He had two weapons: a PSG stunner and a Veer Industries plastic knife. A laughable arsenal by his standards, but of course he had had to keep a low profile to escape. He squeezed the knife in his iron grip, as if flexing his need to kill. He felt half inclined to carve on whomever he found one by one just to pass the time. But he was curious, too, so he decided to talk it out first.

He put away his knife but loosened the clasp holding his stunner in place. Then he climbed a little farther. The wall on his right had a tunnel carved into it. There was a spot for another of the ceramic grates, but the grate had been pulled out and set to one side. He would have to crouch a bit, but the tunnel was clearly passable for Terrans. It had rough red walls with gaps where the rock had split and cracked. DeVries walked into the tunnel.

He heard voices. The urgent rhythm of the hissed whispers told him they had detected him.

"I come in peace," he called out. "I am only one man." His voice echoed ahead. He estimated there must be many chambers and passageways.

"Please leave us be. We're not with the space force," replied someone.

DeVries's heart rate increased.

How could they possibly know I'm concerned about the space force? They can't.

He took a few more steps forward. The outside light filtered in through another of the large gratings in the ceiling of a small, square room. The far side had a low wall built around its corner, which made DeVries think of a well. Four men in robes stood by the wall with blue plastic containers. Two of the men wore reddish robes, the color of the rocks outside, and two of them wore yellow. DeVries had to double check that they were men, wondering if two of them might be women. But they all looked male. Three had short, dark hair. One was bald. The robes made them appear simple, but he reminded himself they could have any kind of equipment under the plain coverings.

"What makes you think I care about the space force?" asked DeVries. His voice was calm, soothing even. He knew most people found his appearance nonthreatening.

"You're their enemy, correct? You're from the UED?"

"No. What makes you think the UED would be here? Oh. You've been cut off, haven't you? United Earth Defiance lost the war."

"That does not concern us. But we have seen UED forces here recently."

"Really?"

"A squadron of marines. We assumed you were one of them."

Wow. Small universe. At least it seems that way when everyone flocks to rocky planets in the habitable zone.

"I'm a free agent," DeVries said carefully. "How about yourselves?"

"We're here for an amazing denizen of this world, the Konuan."

"Never heard of it. Is it valuable? You're hunters?"

"The Konuan. They used to live here by the thousands. Maybe the millions. They created a city here. The water you must have detected is from one of their cisterns."

"What happened to them?"

The man shrugged. "It's another mystery. Like so many other civilizations that fell into dust, on Earth and elsewhere."

"If they're gone, then what do you care about them?"

The man smiled. "The Konuan had their secrets," he said. "Every race has its wisdom. Our sect seeks to collect these insights across all the intelligences in the galaxy. By examining the spiritual knowledge of every race, we can deduce the truths that bind them all together. The truths that are constants in the universe."

Oh. He's a buckle bulb. Thinks he can glean the meta information of the universe by studying the religious beliefs of all races everywhere.

"Their secrets probably died with them," DeVries said, careful not to contradict the fanatic statements.

"There is one left. We serve it," another of the men said.

DeVries looked at the others. Their faces were pinched and weathered. They did not move to deny the statement.

"We are its disciples," echoed another man. He must have seen DeVries looking for repudiation.

Disciples?

"Whoa. You serve it? You've seen it?"

"Yes. You can, too, if you wish. It is amazing," said a bald man, stepping forward carefully.

"What does it look like? Do you talk to it?"

"We're still learning to communicate. It will be happy to see you, if you would like to join us. We can learn together."

"I really just need some water..." DeVries hesitated; then his curiosity got the better of him. "What does it look like?" he asked again.

"You really need to see it for yourself. It can be the size of a man, but it's thin. These vents all around," the man pointed at the ceramic grille above, "are its doorways. It can easily move through them."

DeVries considered the grille again. The spaces were tight. Only his arm could slip through one of the openings. If the creature could slip through there...

"It's like an amoeba? Or is it…rigid? Really that thin?"

"The Konuan is like a moving carpet," said the closest man. "Its underside has a thousand little legs scattered all across it. The top is covered with sensitive antennae and a fine fur."

DeVries nodded. "Are you absolutely sure it's intelligent? The space force wouldn't have made this an open world if they knew there was a sentient creature here."

"Judge for yourself," the bald man said. "Stay and learn with us, if you like."

DeVries felt the touch of fear in his gut when he considered the alien monster, the Konuan. Their description sounded kind of alarming. DeVries didn't like the sound of a thin creature with countless legs on one side of a pancake-flat body. Still, he felt interested in it. He wouldn't have come out to the edge of Terran space without a streak of wonder about the universe.

"Where? You know where it is?"

"Yes. Down below," said the bald one. He pointed to a tunnel. The entrance was ringed in black vegetation. "Past the blackvines."

DeVries stared at the blackvines. His face tightened into a frown. He had seen them once before since landing, growing in the formation that hid his ship. They didn't sit there like proper plants, oblivious to everything around them except the sun. These things were always twitching and keening in response to a passerby or sending tendrils after alien vermin in a nearby crevice. They were presumably blind yet remained aware of things going on around them.

"All right. Are you coming?"

"I will accompany you," the man said, stepping forward.

"You know what? I'd like to check it out myself. Thanks, though," he said. DeVries often tried to avoid traps by doing the opposite of what someone he didn't trust suggested.

Did they lead me into this? Is it a trap?

DeVries looked back at the disciples. They didn't seem nervous. DeVries ran a program in his link. In a split second the link computer examined his cache of the last conversation and analyzed the strangers. The result was encouraging: no hostile intent detected.

DeVries's hand briefly rested on his stunner.

No trap. I'm the predator here. These are sheep.

DeVries steeled himself to the blackvines and walked through.

The tunnel beyond felt truly ancient. Dust and bits of debris littered the smooth tile floor. His nose caught a new smell: a whiff of ammonia.

Maybe the aliens didn't have bathrooms. No, that would be long gone by now. Probably the disciples have been pissing in here somewhere.

The tunnel opened into a large, square room. Like the rest of the place, it was carved from the dusty red rocks. A single ten-liter water container sat in one corner. It was a rugged type of container used by the space force, colonists, and core world survivalists. DeVries saw more of the grilles on each wall and the ceiling. He saw one had been removed to allow him to enter. It leaned against the wall next to the entrance.

This place is locked down tight. Impossible to get anywhere without breaking through those things. And I don't think the grilles were made by humans. The space force wouldn't lock down each room from the other with a thick ceramic barrier. Konuan doors? Maybe that buckle bulb knows at least part of what he's talking about.

The middle of the room held a huge vat. It was a circular depression about two feet deep at the center. The vat was empty except for a few pieces of straight gray debris. DeVries's first thought was of bones. If it was a skeleton of some kind, he decided it probably wasn't human.

Since there was no unblocked exit, DeVries decided to try to remove a grille himself. He approached the one opposite his entrance tunnel. It looked heavy, but apparently the disciples had been opening them up so they could move about in the ruins. DeVries prided himself on his animal strength. It had helped him dispatch many of his victims. He grasped the obstacle and gave an experimental pull. It did not budge.

"Not even close," he said to himself. The grille felt like it was fused in place.

DeVries heard a soft scraping from his right. He turned toward another grille. Suddenly his heart started slamming against his rib cage. He drew the stunner from his belt by reflex. He had long ago disabled its requirements for target logging; the weapon would shoot at anything and everything DeVries ordered it to.

Is that the Konuan?

A yellow line appeared between to bars of the grille. It looked like foam at first; then DeVries saw the edge of it: a black border to the yellow. Dozens of tiny yellow claws grasped the outside edge of one bar, all on one side.

Yes. All its legs are on one side. It's climbing sideways to get through the grille. Must be.

DeVries aimed his stunner. The Konuan shot out of the grille like a whip. It opened to envelop DeVries at the last second. He pulled the stunner's trigger in shock, but the thing was already on him.

Thousands of tiny claws scraped at his head and face. A powerful, acrid smell hit him. Ammonia. He fell back from the impact, losing his balance.

DeVries opened his mouth to scream, but no sound came out. Instead he coughed spasmodically. The ammonia smell was overwhelming. He struck the floor, but he had lost all sense of direction or caring about anything but the need to escape. His hands tore at the outside of the creature covering his torso, but he couldn't get a grip on any part of it. He thrashed violently in the hands of animal panic. His eyes burned. His legs kicked.

Merciful oblivion came seconds later as he lapsed into unconsciousness.

Chapter 1

Magnus sat comfortably in a swivel throne with his feet propped up on an opulent marble desk. Judging from the size and decor of the office that surrounded him, few would have guessed he sat in a spacecraft. The smart chairs arrayed before him adjusted to their occupants and could even serve drinks or drugs. The ceiling rose to twice his height. A shoji screen framed his chair, with scenes from worlds he had visited flitting across its panels.

Vovokans know how to travel in style. Magnus smiled. Given the size of Shiny's house, the huge ship must have seemed tiny to the alien. But to Magnus, it was a flying mansion. And they had all had time to pray up a few amenities for the new transport before they left. A marble statue of Magnus occupied one corner; a similarly beautiful sculpture of Telisa stood in the other. The sculpture caught his imagination and memory for the hundredth time. Since they had been able to pray up almost anything since finding the Trilisk AI, Telisa and Magnus had enjoyed many romantic encounters, both real and virtual.

I wonder how Shiny ever survived being cooped up in the Iridar. *It must have felt like a concentration camp to him. Yet he said nothing.*

He shifted in his seat as a preamble to action. Then he opened an obfuscated channel to Jason Yang. The reply offered Magnus a video and audio feed so he took them both. Jason's face appeared in his mind's eye.

"How's progress?" Magnus asked, getting right to the point.

"I have the three new ships you wanted," Jason said. "The prices were high. The market has been affected by the industrial load of the space force orders for its new grand fleet. We need pilots and crew."

"I'm going to find people for it. I have to figure out where we stand with the local government before I can get back there. But you could help by going ahead and collecting a solid pool of candidates. Hundreds if you want. I can cull them down."

"No sign of anything wrong here," Jason said. "What do they want you for?"

"Trespassing, basically. It was a misunderstanding," Magnus lied.

"Well, with the aliens after us, I doubt they care about you anymore."

"Let's hope so. What do you mean, 'with the aliens after us'?"

"You know, the *Seeker*. The war? You don't follow the news out there?"

"There was an incident. Not a war."

"Then why is every colony making a defense network? Why are the core worlds assembling a grand fleet?"

"Because everyone finally realized there are living aliens out there, not just dead civilizations. But I knew that all along. So did Telisa. It stands to reason. The galaxy is just a big place. Of course, the UNSF loves being able to use it as an excuse to build up."

"You think they made it all up?"

"No…I believe there are live alien civilizations out there."

"But you don't think they are getting ready to attack us?"

"I doubt it. But anything's possible. There's no war yet though, okay?"

"Fair enough," Jason admitted. He actually sounded disappointed.

"You know if there is a war, we'll probably lose, right? We're pretty new to FTL travel."

Jason nodded. "Yeah," he said, getting a bit more serious. "It must be hard, living out there on the frontier,"

Jason said. "There must be few amenities out that far. And you're so removed from everything that's happening."

Jason had no video feed of Magnus, so he couldn't see the interior of the Vovokan ship. Magnus scanned the ultra-luxurious office. He thought of the swimming pool, his workshop, his giant sleep web, and his training center lying just beyond the walls around him.

"Yes, Jason, it's hard. But someone has to be out here, taking the risks, learning what we can. And, of course, making the big finds that are financing the revival of Parker Interstellar Travels."

"Yes! Yes, that's true. You're not afraid the aliens will find you?"

"The aliens?" Magnus echoed distractedly. Then he seemed to return to focus. "By the Five, we're out here *looking* for the aliens!"

Jason nodded. His face showed only idolatry.

"I just need you to hang in there for a while longer until we can return and fire things back up," Magnus continued. "I'll contact you again later this month. For now, just continue your studies and hold down the fort."

"Will do."

Magnus cut the connection. He leaned back in the throne and wondered.

Am I really interested in ever coming back?

***

Telisa received the signal Cilreth had configured to notify everyone of the close approach to Chigran Callnir Four. But the signal was hardly news. She hadn't been able to resist monitoring their status very carefully. Their Vovokan ship was one of two moving together toward the target planet. The Terrans traveled in a ship of their own, which was slaved to the other one with Shiny aboard. Its name was a collection of foot stomps and clacks, so Telisa had christened it simply the *Clacker*. It was an impressive ship, faster, safer, and ten times bigger than *Iridar* had been. Cilreth had been working hard the whole voyage, trying to set up a suite of interfaces the Terrans could use to interact with the alien ship.

My third major expedition. So amazing. I have to pinch myself every time I set foot on a new planet. Could it ever get boring?

Telisa considered the focus of the mission yet again: to find more Trilisk artifacts. Shiny had finally come clean with a translated download of information about the long-gone race.

Telisa had pored over the trove with such intensity that Magnus had started to complain about her lack of training, even though he was almost as obsessed with his new battalion of scout robots. Telisa knew he was right to push her to continue training, but a virtual dossier filled with everything Shiny had managed to accumulate on the Trilisks was perhaps the most interesting read she'd ever possessed.

Shiny's race, which she still called Vovokans, since her naming-on-a-whim had stuck, had been aware of the existence of the Trilisks for hundreds of years. In total, they had encountered Trilisk ruins on no fewer than sixty-three worlds across their entire range of exploration, suggesting that the Trilisks were at one time an incredibly successful race spanning a territory larger than that of the Terrans and the Vovokans put together.

The technology found on these planets had been very challenging for the Vovokans to understand, just as had happened for the Terrans. Some breakthroughs had been made in harnessing or influencing Trilisk devices, but fully controlling or replicating the artifacts had eluded the Vovokans, at least as far as Shiny knew. Unfortunately, intense competition between Vovokans did not foster complete exchanges of information, so Shiny wasn't privy to every advance made in understanding the Trilisks. Like Shiny himself, who had kept the Trilisk AI under wraps and used it to secure his own household, many Vovokans might have had Trilisk items that they utilized in unknown ways to give themselves hidden advantages.

Shiny described Earth's government as a "stagnant monopoly." What Telisa had gleaned of the Vovokan state of affairs made that understandable: she saw the now-defunct government of Vovok as a fluid laissez-faire of overlords in transient alliance where might made right. Shiny claimed such an unstable situation ensured continued gains in intelligence among the populace. He stopped short of proclaiming Terra to be on a backward slide in intellect, but Telisa had taken the hint.

According to Shiny's information, the Trilisks were believed to have mastered problems on the scale of instantaneous travel across great distances, prescience of future events, and immortality. There was evidence they had completely destroyed stars (and thus, their associated planetary systems) in an ancient war with a methane-breathing race of aliens who had become their bitter enemies. That war was the one best answer to the question: Where had the Trilisk civilization gone? If they had won that war, wouldn't they still be here today? And it begged the next question: What was the fate of their enemies?

And now we're going to investigate another ruin of their civilization.

Telisa and Magnus had considered the possibility of looking for the suspected Trilisk outpost in Mesopotamia back on Earth, but flying back into the teeth of an unfriendly government did not seem wise. Magnus had argued that it was pretty clear the outpost was dead, since as Shiny mentioned, supplication had stopped working on Earth long ago.

Telisa had agreed with this point, while at the same time having to argue that they should all stay allied with

Shiny. At first Cilreth and Magnus were all too eager to abandon the alien after their last expedition, but slowly the lavish rewards of their toils had mellowed them out. The plentiful resources, an ability to produce almost anything you could specify carefully enough, and a vast complex of rooms, tools, and technology at their beck and call had softened their suspicions and paranoias. The Vovokan had made good on his promise of providing a new starship, and it was better than their last one in every way. Except perhaps that it would get too much attention at any Terran spaceport. In the end everyone agreed to stay away from Earth for now, remain with Shiny, and embrace the idea of looking at other ruins on the frontier.

Telisa donned her new Veer suit and prepared a personal collection of useful artifacts. She arrayed her equipment before her in the large shipboard room before a giant mirrored wall. Telisa kept her cautious attitude despite the fact that she felt equipped to face a small army and survive. Shiny had downloaded his knowledge of the vault collection, allowing her to separate the alien artifacts into two groups: those for sale and those for her personal collection. The limitations of the Trilisk AI meant there were still things Telisa could not pray up back at their base, and thus still wanted to buy. Besides, as Magnus kept reminding her, they had to fund their front company back at home since it might prove useful if they dared to return to Earth someday.

After long hours of study and several heated discussions with Magnus, Telisa had selected several items for use on the mission.

Feeling more like a warrior every expedition, she had started out with weapons. She chose a tanto, a stunner, and the powerful alien weapon that had saved her life on Vovok, which she called her "chain lightning gun." Though it shot sophisticated projectiles and not any kind of electrical energy, the display it had made in the dark shaft on Vovok had resembled nothing more than a multi-pronged lightning bolt. Shiny had prayed her up a reload for the weapon, which could only hold three shots. But what shots they were!

The next artifact she chose was a cloak system from the Vovokan vault. Telisa had taken a liking to the invisible sphere she had found by accident on one of the shelves. She'd learned how to extend the cloak of the sphere to hide herself. The effect was similar to the special suit her father had taken from a spy. Though she couldn't tell the difference, Shiny assured her the alien stealth sphere was a more complete and durable stealth system than the Terran equivalent. Shiny had easily seen her father in the Terran stealth suit due to his mass signature, but the sphere system was able to block that as well.

Telisa had figured out how to activate the sphere with her link, so she hid it away in her backpack where it could remain safe and serve her as needed.

The next item was another kind of weapon, really, though a highly specialized one. It could be used to deadly effect on large machines. Telisa held the flat piece of metal in her palm. It was shaped like a giant eagle's claw. Exactly why it was that shape probably had more to do with the details of some unknown alien's physiology than anything else. She called it her "breaker claw." It could remotely cause a superconductor to gain resistance. Superconductors were used for many things, including power storage in large robots and machines. When a superconducting storage system suddenly got hit by the breaker, at the very least a lot of power would be wasted, and more likely in many systems was a violent explosion as the stored energy was released in spectacular fashion. Telisa had tested it on one of Magnus's scout robots. The machine had been completely destroyed because it contained a Vovokan power system Magnus had adapted with Shiny's help.

The last two items were identical: tiny spheres. Telisa grabbed them in one hand and gave them a solid upward toss. Instead of arcing up, then falling to the floor, the spheres immediately began to orbit her about half a meter away. They were both Vovokan attendant spheres, gifts from Shiny. The gifts were part of the next "mutually beneficial arrangement" for the expedition. The spheres could not only help to protect her, but they could also be used as spies, scouts, computers, and a long list of other miscellaneous services. Cilreth had taken a liking to them immediately, and a day later she had figured out how the Terrans could integrate the spheres with their links.

Telisa regarded herself in the mirror. The spheres lazily drifted by.

I'm like a superhero with a long list of cool devices stowed away on my utility belt, she thought. *If I can only remember all my amazing superpowers when I need them!*

It was only a half joke. With so many new toys, selecting the right one for her attention under pressure took some getting used to. It was like giving a kickboxer another couple of arms and legs: she would fall back on her originals by instinct but needed to remember the new arsenal. Telisa and Magnus had been training with her new items in VR, trying to integrate them with their combat styles. But it had all been too much, too fast. She still didn't feel comfortable enough to get everything working by reflex.

Maybe there won't be any combat this time, she thought. *Just some digging around and some mysteries to be solved...*

***

Cilreth calmed herself, trying to master feelings of frustration. She struggled with her interface to the ship and demanded a surface scan for the tenth time.

She finally got some unknown parameter correct. Her link filled with data. The next problem presented itself: information overload.

She tried again with a restrictive set of filters. She got a graphical display of the planet and opened it in her personal view.

"Okay, well, what can I see here? No major cities. Good. Progress is progress."

She saw what looked like forests or jungles. A lot of life was catalogued in her scan.

I don't have to struggle by myself for hours to make each little insight. I'll bug Shiny for a minute.

She connected to Shiny aboard his own ship nearby.

"Shiny. I'm trying to understand what I'm seeing from the planet below." She sent the alien the results she'd received from the ship's systems.

"Scan parameters suboptimal," Shiny responded. "Data highly filtered, restricted, limited."

"That part is on purpose. I'm trying to start small and work my way up."

"Understandable. Forgivable. Reasonable."

"Well do you see any threats on the surface?" *Oh wait...is he going to take that too literally?* "And by the surface I mean...do you see any threats on the planet?"

"Affirmative. Millions of threats, dangers, potential sources of harm. All within expected limits, boundaries, ranges. Recommend team proceed with caution."

Cilreth rolled her eyes. "Duly noted."

By next time I'm going to have this thing mastered eight ways from extinction so I can know what the hell I'm getting into.

"Thanks," she said. "What's the name of your ship?"

A series of clacks and thumps came back.

Oh right.

"Ah, I'll call it *Thumper*," she said, continuing Telisa's streak of humor.

Cilreth turned her attention toward the planetary approach. The landing procedure was completely automated, of course. Cilreth had stubbornly looped requirements for her approval into every step, in an effort to become more familiar with the spacecraft. With her approval, the *Clacker* launched its landing "feet" down toward the surface ahead of its descent.

Detachable feet for a spaceship. I never would have thought in a million years...

The landing feet were small metal platforms that arrived ahead of the ship, scouted the area, secured themselves to the surface in a landing geometry that their scans indicated could support the weight of the ship, and then accepted the ship's landing struts. The system enabled the massive bulk of the ship to settle on almost any surface.

She watched a feed from one of the remote feet as a huge sphere of black metal and carbon descended from the sky onto the rocky yet richly vegetated world of Chigran Callnir Four.

When the ship made contact, she had it send out a message to the rest of the crew: Magnus and Telisa.

"We're here. And Shiny says: many dangers, proceed with caution."

I'd better get into my gear. Those two will be out there in no time. She sniffed the air. *It's still not quite right in here. Sigh. Another problem waiting for me when I get back.*

***

A flat metal landing pad detached from the underside of the *Clacker* and established itself below the ship to receive those embarking onto the surface. It was the size of a small building, more than enough to hold the Terrans and their machines. Once the pad settled, three large tubes extended from the belly of the ship. The tubes started to disgorge six-legged scout robots. Each machine had a roughly spherical body with four sensor bulbs spaced across the equator and a weapon mount on the top. Magnus had given the machines a quick spray of red paint to match the rock of the local terrain. The scouts floated gently down onto the detachable landing pad; then they started to move off in all directions.

Telisa emerged from one of the tubes. Like the scout robots, she floated gently down onto the landing pad. She walked toward the edge of the pad as Magnus descended behind her. She took a careful step out onto the surface of the planet.

Magnus stepped out onto the rocky ground next to Telisa. She had a pair of binoculars in her hands. An attendant sphere picked them up and lifted the optical sensor high above the ground. She closed her eyes to see its input clearly in her personal view. It showed a close-up of the remains of old buildings through the alien vegetation. The buildings looked like collections of cubes glued together and made of a homogenous material of the same color as the reddish rocks. She judged they might be constructed in a manner similar to adobe or brick houses.

"So this is how it's going to be?" Magnus said. "We come down here and hoof around, taking all the risks, while High Lord Shiny looks down on us from orbit?"

Magnus put on an air of frustration, but Telisa saw through it. He was just complaining for the sake of complaining. She knew he was actually as excited as she was to be back on the ground on a new world.

"Think of him as our rich employer," Telisa said. Magnus laughed.

A small army of scout machines explored the area around them. Magnus had brought an even twenty of them to map the landscape ahead of any in-person exploration. The *Clacker*'s vast cargo bays held ten more in reserve. The new scout robots used Vovokan power plants and mass detectors, allowing them to operate for weeks without recharge and giving them the capability to see through walls and other obstacles. Their legs were also much stronger, as Magnus had given them each six legs modeled after those on Shiny's walking machine.

It almost takes the fun out of it, Telisa thought. *If there's any alien nasties, though, better a scout than me.*

"I'm already seeing tunnels under the ground from the scout feeds," Magnus noted.

"Tunnels? Damn. We barely made it out of the tunnels last time," Telisa said.

Magnus shrugged. "Underground habitations survive better across long periods of time. I'd get used to it."

Telisa sighed. She heard a sound behind her. She turned and saw nothing, until Cilreth materialized from thin air.

"Sorry, just testing," she said. Cilreth wore the stealth suit.

"You better not have been using that thing to get a peek into my shower tube," Telisa joked.

Cilreth had made it clear during the voyage that she preferred women, though with Telisa already in a monogamous relationship with Magnus it hadn't impacted the group's dynamic much if at all.

"Oh, I have spy programs for that," she said.

Telisa smiled. She noticed Cilreth had a stunner on one hip and a machete sheathed on the other. *Our weapons fetish has already spread.*

"I guess it's up to us to find out what we can with the scouts. Shiny didn't know much except he swears this used to be a Trilisk planet," Magnus said.

"Well, he said it used to have Trilisks on it," Telisa corrected.

"So, I did manage to get a scan off from orbit," Cilreth said. "According to the *Clacker,* there aren't any major settlements, at least not at any level of technology we'd notice. The interface still needs some work. I know the ship has to be capable of more thorough searches; I just can't operate it well enough yet."

And it's so damn advanced I can barely find my own location marker in it.

"Any information is better than none," Telisa said.

"So, anyway, I was kinda rushed with that work and didn't get a chance to learn about the planet from Terran sources," Cilreth continued.

"I didn't find much on this planet anyway except that it's one of the open worlds," Telisa said. "It says there was a group of creatures here called the Konuan. Now extinct. Some kind of primitive culture. Shiny, are you sure Trilisks were here?"

Shiny joined the channel they shared, presumably at Telisa's invitation. "Certain, verified, known. Ruins around you contain traces of Trilisk presence."

"They may have been here because of the Konuan," Telisa said. "They may have been studying them. Or conquering them. Or whatever it is the Trilisks did."

Cilreth could tell from the edge in Telisa's voice that her companion didn't like being in the dark about the Trilisk's modus operandi.

"Let's get in there and find out what they did," Magnus said enthusiastically.

Michael McCloskey

Chapter 2

The smart screen above the camp flexed gently in a light morning breeze. The screen lay just below most of the green clumps that terminated the stalks, about three meters above the rocky ground. Soldiers worked under the screen. The thin, translucent fabric contained a network of sensors and emitters that scattered their radiation signatures, providing excellent camouflage from orbit. The camp adjoined an escarpment where two square tunnel entrances had been put into the rock. Some men moved in and out of the tunnels while others rested in tents that shifted color lazily to match the densest part of the alien flora above.

Colonel Lance Holtzclaw stood in the center of his camp. This had been home for seven long months. Long enough to become familiar with a place. Long enough to hate a place.

Holtzclaw scratched his infernal itch for the thousandth time. He had started to leave his armored suit open at the front so he could slip his hand in to scratch the pink skin where his replacement arm had been grafted on.

Dammit. What did they do, put someone else's arm on me? Why does it still itch so much?

He glanced at the graft site on his shoulder. The skin of his new arm had proven more aggressive than his old skin. It had grown out from the old line between his new arm and the stump, taking over the original skin of his shoulder. A star-shaped scar still held on at the edge of his chest where part of the seeker round that had taken off his arm had flown out of him.

Maybe they did too good of a job selecting cells to seed the arm. That skin is just healthier than the rest. It's going to take over my whole body…and itch me insane the entire time.

"Colonel," a soldier addressed him, saluting.

Holtzclaw took a deep breath. "Yes?"

"I've picked up activity in the atmosphere. A big ship. It landed on the other side of the ruin, down past the broken spire."

"Any chance it's one of ours?"

"No, sir. It's got to be space force. The signature is nothing civilian, nothing like I've seen anyway, and it's really big."

Just when you thought things couldn't get any worse.

"Tell Silvarre and get him to the Hellrakers," Holtzclaw ordered. The soldier rushed off.

Holtzclaw opened a channel to his perimeter captain as he hustled to the artillery. "Possible incoming," he said. "I'm showing up at HR-2 for an inspection. Double check the perimeter drones."

"Yes, sir."

"Are all the Guardians active?"

"Yes, sir, though Shredder—that is, number five—has only seventy rounds. It's on the north side."

Holtzclaw nodded. It was as he remembered. He simply wanted to double-check everything and get everyone ready for the worst. If the UNSF was here, chances were it wouldn't be a minor attack.

Hellraker number two sat beside one of the largest alien plants in the camp. The men called it Thor. The robotic artillery piece was in the best shape of the four Hellrakers his unit had once operated. One of the four had been cannibalized for a few parts too sophisticated for their assault ships to fabricate. The other two were operable though compromised in one way or another. Thor was just about perfect. It was a treaded vehicle, five meters on a side, taller than Holtzclaw, and covered in dull black armor with a group of four stub barrels pointed at the sky.

With the help of the spotting drones, or any other accurate information source, the machine could deliver anti-personnel shells to any location within thirty kilometers. The smart shells it launched were rocket/projectile hybrids. They were also highly configurable and could alter their own course enough to change the destination by kilometers on the way down. They could also be directionalized to deliver more power in a particular direction upon impact. The kill radius of each smart shell when the blast was evenly distributed extended over one hundred meters.

The Hellrakers could launch two shells per second (though the one dubbed Conan had to fire more slowly), which was often useful for saturating defenses. The Hellrakers were their only real chance of fighting back if the UNSF had found them. Though with only three machines left, Holtzclaw knew any engagement with space force robots could be disastrous for him and his unit. They were simply running too low on men, machines, parts, and ammunition.

The fourteen Guardian robots on their perimeter could buy them time, but those machines were old and had limited range. As soon as any sophisticated fighting unit acquired them, the Guardian's lifespan would be measured in seconds. To make matters worse, the space force usually fought with support from orbit.

Silvarre showed up ten seconds after Holtzclaw. Silvarre had short charcoal hair and a deep tan. Holtzclaw's highest ranked subordinate looked lean compared to the solid block of Holtzclaw's square body. The man's cheeks looked more sunken. Holtzclaw thought Silvarre looked worse than when he last saw him, but said nothing.

Holtzclaw thought about their other ordnance. He had four lightly armed assault ships, designed to carry his men from world to world. The ships had been able to produce just enough food and parts to keep them going. He could scramble those and try to attack the enemy ship while they were on the ground. If the UNSF was conducting an armed drop, though, there would be other ships in orbit prepared to interdict.

More men started to arrive.

"Crack open the backup magazines," Holtzclaw ordered. The men obeyed, showing him the reloads they had waiting for the artillery machine. Silvarre and Holtzclaw examined what they could and ran some diagnostics while their UED remote sensor probes waited for signs of an incoming attack.

Fifteen minutes ticked by with no sign of the enemy. If the space force came, he would order his officers to disperse, have the link jamming turned on, and bolster the defense. They saw only the red rocks pocked with holes, the tall alien plants, and the old buildings of the Konuan ruins. All their scans, electromagnetic, seismic, and chemical, indicated nothing amiss.

"They must not know we're here," Silvarre said. "There would be no reason to hold back after a drop in the open like that."

"Then why are they here? This isn't exactly a point of strategic interest. And they've won the war, at least for now."

"It's time to reexamine our assumption that it's the space force," Holtzclaw said.

"Whoever they are, maybe the damn monster will get them," Silvarre said.

"It'll get a few of them, sure," Holtzclaw said. "Then they'll get wise and start hunting it. Unlike us, they're bound to have plenty of supplies to use against it."

Which means we should make their supplies our supplies, he thought.

"Maybe it's just a big science expedition," Silvarre suggested. "We could take 'em."

"Hang low. Maintain surface camouflage discipline. We're getting close to some of the inner chambers. I'd like to see if we can find what we want before they notice us."

"Yes, sir."

"Send out a couple of probes under cover of darkness. Don't let them get too close, you hear me? Set up some surveillance about a kilometer out from where they touched down."

"Yes, sir…" Silvarre hesitated. "It's going to be a dicey night here without those sensor probes, sir."

Silvarre referred to the monster that hunted them. They had just enough detection to make it challenging for the creature to hunt them. Every now and then a scout probe spotted the thing and recruited a nearby Guardian to take a few shots at it. When that happened it usually retreated.

"I know it. But we won't be here much longer. Either we're going to get out of here, or we're going to hit them and take everything they have. Just sleep with your finger on the trigger tonight."

Silvarre nodded grimly.

Maybe we'll get lucky and blast the monster's brains out this time. Or maybe it will find easier prey across the ruins.

The next hour drew itself out slowly, agonizingly. Holtzclaw finally decided no attack was coming. He left men at the ready by Thor just in case. He went down into the tunnels to check on progress. The arrival of the strange ship meant the schedule had to be accelerated even further.

He entered the room near the heart of the Trilisk complex, or at least the spot they had decided had the most promise. Men worked all around him.

We're already working as fast as we can, he told himself. *You can't make it any faster. You just can't.*

The room had been enlarged, though it had cost them dearly. The Trilisk walls were strong, amazingly strong, and self-healing. After a few failed attempts, the UED soldiers had placed large steel columns around the room and slowly jacked up the ceiling after they had cleared the stone above the room from the outside. They cut the ceiling and held it open with cables. Then the Trilisk columns inside were pried from their mounts. All three columns would be removed together, as they were still attached to each by several umbilical lines of varying thickness. No one knew what the lines were for or how they could be disconnected.

A heavy lifting robot stood ready to carry the Trilisk machines. Parts of the robot had been stripped down and reconfigured to fit down into the tunnel. Everything had been a struggle from the beginning. Yet it had given the men purpose, and hope.

It is as if the entire tunnel system was just grown in place, all in one piece by nanomachines, one of his engineers had said. Having to take out the columns by themselves had been like trying to remove a brain intact from its skull with a few wooden sticks.

The whole time, as they had worked feverishly in the tunnels, the monster had been hunting them. Extracting these devices had been their last hope. The scientifically inclined among them had chosen these columns carefully. They had said one was a power source. A staggeringly powerful one. No one knew what the other two columns were, but sitting next to that power they must be important. Possibly weapons or defense of some kind. And that was all they knew.

Forty-three lives lost, and a good part of our sanity, and we don't even know what we're stealing.

Holtzclaw wondered what he had done to anger the Five Entities in a previous life.

Chapter 3

The trio of Terrans followed their scouts toward the center of the ruins around them. Magnus and Telisa eagerly took the lead, while Cilreth was content to follow behind. The rocks were ridged and sharp, clearly not worn by weather as they would have been on many other habitable planets. Cilreth couldn't spot a speck of dirt or even one dead leaf; just the red rocks, the greenish clumps atop their stalks, and the blue sky.

I'd probably be more useful back on the Clacker, *trying to figure it out,* Cilreth thought as she picked her way over the rough terrain. *But after being stuck in there, it's nice to get out and see a new world.*

Cilreth had discovered that even a huge ship was still an enclosed microenvironment. She often roamed through virtual worlds, which fed her advanced mind, but some primitive instinct in her brain still cried out for a real planetary surface.

"What do you think?" asked Telisa, bubbling with enthusiasm.

"I can see why you enjoy it," Cilreth said neutrally.

"You like it, too," Telisa said. "The excitement of checking out a fresh, new world!"

"Yeah, well, so far so good, but where's the dirt? The leaves? And Shiny said there were dangerous things here."

Telisa shrugged. "I don't know. We can find out."

Something made a noise to their right. It sounded like a clicking or grinding on the rocky ground. Telisa raised her weapon. "Magnus."

"Telisa," Magnus replied and turned. Telisa indicated the direction of the noise.

"Check your feeds," Magnus said, turning away. "That's one of ours."

"Shit," Telisa said. Cilreth checked her own scout information and finally found the one Magnus had mentioned.

He's good at that. Must be military training.

The scout robot came into view, checking the dark holes in nearby rocks with a measuring laser and an ultrasonic probe. Cilreth checked its data. The larger plants it had investigated had created underground fissures in the rock filled with softer material. She thought all the surface particulates might have been washed into the resulting holes.

Self-made plant pots?

Telisa and Cilreth walked after Magnus. The first of the ancient houses they found were broken open and destroyed. Cilreth thought of them as houses because they were small and isolated on the outskirts of the ruins. The structures were always cubical. Each house held the rubble of its own broken walls and ceiling. Nothing had really survived on the surface of the original furniture or decor, if there ever was any. They continued on toward denser groups of buildings visible on the hillsides ahead, jutting above the strange plants that grew from every crevice in the rocks.

The plants had thick trunks like bamboo plants, but they quickly split into three branches that in turn split into three again. Each branch then terminated in clumps of greenish material three or four meters above the ground. Each clump looked like moss or hair. The effect was odd; in fact, if they hadn't been on an alien planet, Cilreth might have suspected herself to be in a children's VR.

She spotted a flash of bright red on a plant stalk.

"Wait, stop, I see something," Cilreth said.

Telisa turned back to look. Cilreth pointed at the red shape wrapped around an alien plant. The plant stood more or less alone amid a pile of spiky reddish rock.

It's probably just a flower and you're making an idiot of yourself.

Magnus turned as well. He pointed his rifle and backtracked the way he'd come. Cilreth glanced around to see if anything else looked odd while she pulled out her stunner. Soon Magnus had interposed himself between Cilreth and the plant where she'd glimpsed movement.

Typically male of him to step to the fore as if he has to protect us. But it makes sense, too; he is the most experienced with dangerous environs.

"I see it," Telisa said. The nebulous red shifted. It was hard to follow. "But it's hard to track. I feel like there's something wrong with my eyes when I look at it."

Whatever it was reared up from the plant it encircled. It emitted a half hiss, half buzz. Cilreth saw the creature was partially transparent. Once armed with that knowledge, what she saw started to make more sense.

"It's mostly transparent. That red part is…inside," she said. "You're pissing it off."

Telisa kept glancing behind herself, though Cilreth couldn't see why. Magnus stepped back.

"Perhaps best avoided," he said; then the creature attacked.

The red ribbon of color coiled then launched itself at Magnus. It seemed certain to connect with him, yet it fell short and to one side. Its impossible trajectory confused Cilreth for a second.

What? Oh. A Vovokan sphere intercepted it.

Magnus staggered back a step. Telisa didn't hesitate. She was at his side in a flash, her tanto drawn.

"Back slowly," he said. His voice was rock steady.

Crap, he's calm.

Cilreth had access to his vitals as an expedition member, but she didn't have time to check at the moment. The creature launched itself again. This time three of the orbiting spheres, two from Magnus and one from Telisa, intercepted the line of flight and deflected the sinuous attacker.

Magnus leveled his weapon and fired it once. The creature started to whip wildly back and forth across the rocks. The Terrans backed away, then resumed their previous course. The creature had been injured or at least cowed. Cilreth lost sight of the thing as it struggled.

"I assume that will be a fatal wound, unless it's a particularly tough creature," Cilreth said.

"How did you spot it?" Telisa asked. "I didn't see anything when I went by."

"I don't know. Just caught sight of the red, just for a moment. Why did you keep looking behind yourself back there?"

Telisa looked surprised by her question. "On Vovok, we encountered a few mostly harmless creepy crawlies. But dealing with a few brought lots more. We kind of stirred up a hornet's nest. I guess I'm paranoid about it happening again. Of course I know, different planet, different dangers."

"Makes a lot of sense. You're learning from your experiences." *Or failing to get over your bad experiences*, thought Cilreth's cynical side.

"I keep telling myself I'll get used to it like Magnus," Telisa said. Magnus ignored the conversation, as he was checking some input in his link. Cilreth checked his recent biomarkers through her link. She was a little encouraged to see his heart rate had increased 20 percent. Telisa's had increased a bit more, while her own had skyrocketed along with her adrenal spike.

He's human, at least.

"A scout found something interesting," Magnus announced.

Cilreth had access to the many roving eyes of the scouts, but she found it hard to concentrate on her own movements across the rough terrain and watch the scout feeds at the same time. Cilreth loved the machines intellectually, though the way they moved creeped her out. She did not much care for Magnus's PV interface to them either, though that was hardly surprising given that Magnus was not as experienced with software as she was.

Magnus led them toward another ancient building. The structure looked to be in better shape than the outlying ruins. They walked up to an intact reddish wall. One of the scout robots crawled nearby.

The stone wall held a thick ceramic grille or window at the level of Cilreth's stomach. She estimated it to be a little over a meter square. Its color looked slightly more brownish than the red rock surrounding it.

"So what is it?" Cilreth asked. "A vent, I think."

Telisa took out a light and shined it through. "There's a room beyond. Mostly empty from what little I can see. There's another vent like this on the far wall, but that one doesn't look like it could lead directly outside."

"I don't see any other entrances. We can skip it and check another spot."

"But this building is intact," Telisa persisted. "Maybe this is a door. It looks like a vent to us."

"Great door it must have been. It's full of holes."

"Maybe they needed ventilation. Maybe the weather is always good."

Magnus checked the grille for opening mechanisms. His hands went around the perimeter of the vent, pressing and prodding.

"It feels solid," he said. He took out his own light and checked beyond, then grabbed the ceramic lattice and pulled.

"Either wedged or solid as designed," he said. "This wall is old, though. I think we could force our way in."

The scout robot approached. Magnus stood back, so Cilreth backed away, too. The spider robot started to attack the wall with the sharp tips of its front legs. Each time it whipped a leg into the wall, a chunk of material fell away. The little craters accumulated until a deep, crumbling hole grew at one corner of the grille. Cilreth was impressed at the strength of the Vovokan-designed legs. The scout robot was strong.

"Something odd is happening around the corner here," Magnus said. He held his rifle ready in his hands, though his voice was calm.

"What?" Telisa asked. Cilreth followed them to the corner of the building with Magnus in the lead. When she turned the corner, Cilreth saw the red rocks on the ground were covered with creeping green worms. Hundreds of them.

"Whoa! What are those?"

"They're coming from that tree thing," Telisa observed. Cilreth followed the same visual trail as Telisa. More of the green, caterpillar-like bugs were running down a stalk from the dissolving green blob at the top of the stalk.

"Wait a sec, are they coming from the plant—or maybe they *are* the plant!" Cilreth said. The creatures were exactly the same color as the green pom-pom–like mass of the leaves. She looked closer. The entire mass left at the end of the stalk writhed.

"Well, I guess our assumptions that these are like Earth plants is off," Magnus said.

"Yes, neither plant nor animal, the distinction may be irrelevant here," said Telisa.

Magnus kicked one away as it neared his foot. The green worm did not appear to have any legs, though it reminded her of a furry caterpillar.

"Dangerous?" asked Cilreth. *We walked right by dozens of those green clumps. I walked under several.*

"Doesn't look bad," Telisa said.

"Neither do army ants, at first," Magnus said. "Besides, it's alien and we have no idea. Let's head back to the opening."

"What do you think it's doing? Or should I say they?" asked Cilreth.

"Maybe that spot ran out of nutrients," Telisa suggested. "Or maybe it hunts that way. Maybe we should grab a sample?"

"Good idea," Cilreth said. She took a small container from her pack. She put the trap in front of one, encouraging it to slide inside. Just in case, she held the clear plastic so her hand was shielded by the container. Magnus watched the entire operation intently. The capture was uneventful. Cilreth captured another one and then sealed the container.

They turned around and put space between themselves and the expanding ring of worms. Magnus stared at her captive creatures for a moment.

"Let's leave the container out at camp for a while. Make sure those things can't get out of that."

Cilreth nodded. "Good idea," she said.

"I'll never look at those trees the same again," Telisa said, checking the horizon. "There must be billions of them. What if they all crawl off the stalks at once?"

"Then we're getting the hell out of here," Magnus said. "Maybe I need a flamethrower module for the scout robots."

Telisa laughed and Cilreth joined in.

"What? I'm just trying to be prepared," Magnus said.

"Now, where were we?" Telisa said, walking back toward the building's grille.

The scout machine had made good progress on the opening. Magnus ordered the scout back with his link. Then he stepped forward and grabbed the exposed corner. With a huge heave, he ripped the vent from the wall.

"So much for the door. If it ever was one," Cilreth said. "Who's first?"

But Magnus was already crawling through. Telisa followed with Cilreth in the rear again.

Some ambient light already filtered in through another vent from above as well as the open hole behind them. Cilreth took out her own light to get a better look.

A series of metal frames were set into the floor, three of the walls, and the ceiling. The frames held old metal machines with gears and rods, but no wires. The only empty wall lay toward the outside where they had forced their way in.

Cilreth shined her light on one of the metal frames on the floor before her. At first glance they all looked to be the same type of machine. Four metal struts rose from the floor to secure the one she examined.

"Okay. I can't place this thing. But it's simple, primitive," Cilreth thought aloud.

"Yes. Something was being rolled through it, or around it. Paper? Cloth? It could be a place where pre–electronic age books were created, or a clothing factory."

Cilreth looked at Magnus. He shrugged. "As you say. Something rolled or pressed. Could also have made wire or thin metal foils, or could have been used to squeeze water or liquid out of something. This is not very advanced stuff, unless some of the machines have rotted away and we're just looking at the structural skeletons that remain."

"They made good use of the space," Telisa noted, looking over the same machines hanging from the ceiling.

"Yeah, they're mounted everywhere, even the ceiling," Cilreth agreed.

"Any other first impressions?" Magnus asked. He looked toward Telisa.

"These grilles lead out in all directions," Telisa said. "So unless this is a prison, or mausoleum or something, they must be doorways."

"Then why are they all fused closed?"

"The dimensions of the doorways are considerably smaller than the room. Our own doors are relatively tall. The creatures must be the size of those grilles."

"But the grilles are solidly in place. I'm not so sure they're doors."

"If we can see where that one goes, we might find out," Telisa said. She pointed toward the one opposite their break-in spot.

Magnus knelt before the grille on the far wall and shined his light through the vents. "There's another open space through it. Large." He set the light down and grasped the grille with his gloved hands. He tensed his bulky frame. "It's not moving either. Could it be electronically locked?"

"I don't think so," Cilreth said. "Hrm. I shouldn't be too quick to judge, though. Maybe." She pulled off her equipment pack and set it on the ground. "We can scan it. Or we could break one into pieces and look for evidence of internal workings. Though if sufficiently advanced, it may not be obvious to the naked eye."

"This place doesn't look very advanced to me," Magnus said.

"You never know. This could be their barn, or something a bit older," Telisa said.

"Perhaps the grille moved directly up or sideways, instead of opening like a basic door," Cilreth suggested. "There could be a hidden latch. It's probably easy to open; we just don't know how to do it."

"The outside one had no cavity to slide into," Magnus said. "So if that theory is correct, it must not hold for the outside ones." They examined the grille for a few minutes. No one could find any trick to spring it open.

Magnus stared at the grille before him. "I think this is a time for a primitive approach. A crowbar might work."

"What's that?" Telisa asked.

Cilreth smiled. "An old mechanic's trick from simpler times. Nothing more than a bar of metal to use as a lever. You packed one?"

"No," Magnus admitted. He stood and remained still for a moment. Then a scout robot clambered in, presumably summoned by Magnus. The machine took his place by the grille and started to chip away at the wall. It came away in chunks.

Cilreth walked back around the room while they waited for the machine to dig. The place smelled musty. She tried to imagine what it had looked like new. The grilles made it feel like a prison. An outer layer of the wall had fallen away. It must have been very smooth and could have been some color other than the red stone behind.

Magnus pulled the grille away and tucked it between two of the machines. He scoffed, "Once again, the wall is softer than the grille!"

"Just age," Telisa guessed. The scout machine walked through the resulting hole. They crawled through after it.

The next room's basic architecture was identical to the first. Grilles sat in the center of walls, floor, and ceiling. Metal bars with circular holes extended half a meter from the walls in a dozen places. Two oxidized metal tables with six legs sat on the floor. One more identical structure was affixed to the wall to Cilreth's right.

"What's that stuff? There are…mounts or rods or something on the ceiling, too," Magnus said.

"And the walls. I can't guess what this stuff is," Cilreth said.

"Maybe something used to be suspended in this room, like a sleep web. Maybe it rotted," Magnus said.

"I have a different theory," Telisa said. "This reinforces something I was suspecting earlier. Remember, there were grilles leading in all eight directions from a cubical room, including up and down. Now you see all this along all the walls?"

"These creatures used all the walls and ceiling, maybe even equally," Cilreth said.

"Exactly."

Magnus looked up at the ceiling. "You mean, they...stuck to the walls? Hung upside down?"

"I don't know yet. But these things, whatever they were, utilized all six walls of these rooms in a more equal way. Terrans focus on the floor, install cabinets or equipment into the walls, and practically ignore the ceiling. But here, doors lead out in all six directions. They must have clung to the walls and thus made use of the entire room in ways that wouldn't occur to Terrans."

"Great. A race of banana slugs," Cilreth said.

"Well, that is actually one possibility," Telisa said. "They may have been smaller creatures that stuck to the walls like slugs."

Magnus made a face. "But we're here after the Trilisks."

"That doesn't mean I can't learn a thing or two from the Konuan," Telisa said.

"It looks to me that they were primitive. Iron Age–ish, or whatever passes for iron around here," Cilreth said. She checked the data on the planet again.

Given the density of this planet, iron is likely quite common.

"Yeah," Telisa agreed. "That does make them less interesting from a standpoint of cool goodies to lift. But we need to rethink this city of theirs. If they use all six walls for stuff, then in a way this city is two or three times denser than an equivalent-sized Terran city, right?"

"Hrm. Could be," Magnus said. "Shiny said the Trilisks were here, so let's keep moving."

"What about the scouts? Aren't they supposed to take the heat for us?" Cilreth asked.

"Right now, they can't get through these grilles," Magnus said. "We're going to have to figure out a good way to get through them ourselves. Then I can try and adapt the method to the scouts."

"Well, they have grenades," Telisa said.

"Out of the question," Magnus replied.

"Okay, then, scratch the flamethrowers. It's time to deploy crowbars to your advanced alien robot fleet!" Telisa said. She suppressed a giggle. Magnus shot her a look.

"Well, we need to come up with something, or it's going to take weeks to move through the city," Cilreth said.

"The *Clacker* can fabricate a wide range of tools. Or perhaps the scouts just need a tweak to their methods. I'll figure it out," Magnus said.

Chapter 4

Captain Jamie Arakaki knelt to the rocky ground, allowing her to see farther. The native plants obstructed her view less in their lowest meter where they were mostly naked stalks. More importantly, the kneeling position allowed her to spot the cleargliders from a distance, because the transparent creatures always waited with their tails hanging to the ground. They liked to tease the smaller critters out of the plant wells with their opaque red tails, then drop to attack.

Arakaki didn't spot any cleargliders in the patch. She came back to full standing position. Her dark hair had been tied back to keep it out of her eyes. She periodically chopped off the growing tail of hair with a machete to keep it from getting tangled in anything. She was a compact 1.7 meters of wiry muscle. She wore a combat suit. Its surface changed colors slowly. At the moment it displayed a moody maroon that matched the rocks underfoot.

She walked through the patch of vegetation with a small personal assault weapon in her hands, its empty holster at her hip. A laser dangled at her other hip.

Her destination, a long tent, became visible just ahead. It was a remote tent, placed to gather together small items from the nearby tunnels and evaluate their worth before bringing them back to the assault ships. Arakaki was one of the few people who would make the trip out to the farthest tent alone. No one else actually *wanted* to be attacked by an alien monster.

She heard sounds of movement inside. The PAW she held detected a target signature within. She listened to verify it was a human. The occasional swear word or a clearing of a throat would do it. She froze to listen. Even the sliver of tough plastic she chewed on stopped its idle trip between her teeth, sticking straight out from her thin lips under a canine. After a half minute she heard a long sigh followed by the smack of skin on skin, as of someone slapping away a local bug. Then Arakaki padded up to the entrance, giving the area a last look-over. Her feet didn't make a sound on the jagged rock. She glanced inside, seeing a lone UED soldier at work at a low folding table. Then she slid gracefully inside.

"What've you got for me, Ace?"

The man froze, then smiled. "Nice to finally be apprised of your presence," he said mildly. He looked at the pistol sitting on the table next to him as if to say, *A lotta help that did me.*

"I don't know what they are, but there's four of them, identical, all Trilisk for sure," he continued, pointing at a black pack.

Arakaki pounced on the bag, then hefted it up to her shoulder energetically. She tipped to one side under the weight. Ace caught sight of the move from the corner of his eye.

"Damn, Arakaki, you're nothing but guns and gristle," he said, not turning to look straight on.

"If something's gonna eat me, it's going to have to chew a long time," she said.

The soldier laughed. "I'll chew on you a while," he offered.

"Next time for sure. Right now, I gotta go," she said, leaving the tent without looking back.

Within twenty paces of the tent, she checked the probes for the latest scans on the Konuan.

Three hits last night around three a.m. It probably won't show until late afternoon, she thought.

The creature that hunted them liked to take a crack at the UED soldiers every single day, though it was often turned back. It seldom returned twice in one day and typically separated its hunts by at least ten or twelve hours.

Arakaki wondered if it slept or simply had other tasks on its plate.

But the biggest secret about the Konuan was simply how it had survived at all, when as far as she could tell, every other Konuan had died decades ago at least. Holtzclaw kept saying there could be a handful left, but Arakaki felt it in her gut: there was just one. And it loved to hunt them. To toy with them.

The weight of the pack bit into her shoulders. It would be a long walk back. Holtzclaw's surviving techies would gush over the new pieces, she felt sure.

If you told them a Trilisk pissed on it, they'd rush to examine it.

Not that she knew if Trilisks urinated or not. But she felt that she would probably never find out, and it was just as well, since the aliens had died out and left the galaxy to the Terrans.

It may have found the best Trilisk stuff for itself. That could explain it, she realized. She hadn't considered the possibility before. But if anything could explain a single long-lived Konuan that could sneak in and out of their perimeter and hunt down heavily armed men and women, it was Trilisk technology in its possession.

Goddamn thing. I'm gonna blow it to bits.

Her hand found the smooth black grenade dangling around her throat on a tough nylon line.

Or if it gets me first, I'm taking it with me.

Arakaki had rigged the grenade to a pH sensor so it would detonate if covered in a strong acid. She believed the victims were dissolved by acid secreted by the creature, and the strong ammonia smell was due to bases it used to neutralize the acid once the victim was incapacitated. Whether the ammonia neutralized acid in the victim as potential food or simply kept the creature from dissolving itself from the inside out, she did not know, but every dead soldier had been found with his or her head half gone. If the Konuan got past her eternal vigilance and pounced on her head, it was in for a surprise.

Arakaki moved through the now-familiar old buildings of the original sentient inhabitants of Chigran Callnir Four. Though she had found the empty silence of the ruins unsettling at first, she felt at home among them now, even knowing she could be hunted down and killed. She had made friends with the danger. She bit down on the sliver in her mouth. In fact, she was a bit too eager for danger now, since she had lost him. Some days, she wanted it to end so she didn't have to think about it even one more time.

An hour later it was early afternoon. She had made steady progress through the empty city. Still probably too early for the Konuan to show.

Probably.

She approached the danger zone of the UED perimeter. Arakaki took up a position beside a Konuan building, facing a distant hillside overlooking the ruins. She sent her code from her link to a directional transmitter in her combat suit.

The probe on the distant hillside received her safe entrance request. Somewhere up ahead, a Guardian machine verified her target signature on its no-shoot list.

Arakaki continued. She was still cautious; a clearglider could have wandered into the zone, but more importantly, she wasn't sure enough of the Konuan's habits to risk her life by being careless now.

She came across the Guardian less than a kilometer from the outside of the zone. The machine didn't move. It towered above her on metal spider legs, about twice her height. It had four arms to match its four legs. The arms were weapon mounts. Each arm of number four, or Scorn as the mechanics called it, held a long cannon barrel counterbalanced by an ammunition magazine.

"Welcome back, Captain," Scorn said.

"Any kills today, Scorn?" Arakaki asked, though she could just as easily have checked its fire record directly with her link.

"No kills today, Captain," it told her.

"Me neither," she said, and continued into the camp.

Michael McCloskey

Chapter 5

Magnus awakened to an alert in his PV. At first he thought he had misconfigured his scout leverage analysis to send an important alert when it completed. But it was not related to his project to enable the scouts to pry open the Konuan grilles. It was a warning that one of the machines had been disabled or destroyed.

He opened his eyes. Everything appeared calm within the tent. Their equipment boxes formed parallel walls supporting the tough fabric ceiling. Underneath, a level foam floor protected them from the jagged rocks. Telisa and Cilreth looked asleep, but Telisa sent him a message with her link.

"Something wrong?"

"We've lost a scout," Magnus reported. "It's not near here. Probably nothing to worry about. The machine may have just fallen into a hole or gotten itself into a dumb spot."

Telisa opened her eyes and sat up. She dialed up a cold lantern with her link, bathing the space in more light. "Are we in danger?"

"I don't think so," Magnus said. "The scout we lost was a kilometer out. We still have several local."

The group had discussed sleeping back in the *Clacker*, in the tent amidst their equipment containers, or in the Konuan buildings. Magnus didn't trust the Konuan buildings. Cilreth feared predators and made the case for a trek back to the *Clacker*. In the end, no one had strong objections to setting up inside a ring of equipment and cargo cases for some light shelter.

Magnus's mention of the local scouts was verified by the sounds of tapping coming from the nearest Konuan building. They had left two scouts inside to clear more grilles as they slept. Magnus looked over a few images of the inside.

"Or maybe something nasty got a hold of it," Cilreth said, joining the conversation late.

"Sorry to wake you. It's probably nothing."

"We lost a scout. I'm on a strange alien planet sleeping in a flimsy tent about a kilometer from something nasty. It's not nothing."

Magnus shrugged. "We'll have to investigate at first light. Why don't you stay here and expand our camp? Deploy the rest of our equipment."

Cilreth gave him an inscrutable look. "Okay," she said.

It will be good for her to get used to working out here alone, Telisa said to Magnus over a private channel.

Alone? he replied. *I thought you would stay with her. No way.*

The three played with sleep for another hour and a half, but everyone simply tossed and turned, waiting for daybreak. At the first sign of the Chigran Callnir star above the horizon, Magnus and Telisa eagerly threw together some equipment. Magnus told the tent walls to retract with his link. The morning air was cool but not cold in his Veer skinsuit.

"We'll be back. You've got half a dozen scouts are in this area; call on them if you encounter any more of those transparent snakes, or anything else."

"Got it," Cilreth said. "You guys be careful. If something can kill one of those robots…"

Then it can kill us.

Magnus pulled his rifle off his back and checked it manually and electronically. He loved the old weapon and considered it rock solid. He understood it well enough to obtain more parts and ammunition back at the base through supplication to the Trilisk AI.

Telisa locked on to the destroyed scout herself. She led the way. Magnus followed along while asking two more scouts to converge with them at the site of the attack.

She's eager. Still very cautious, though. A woman after my own heart.

"When are you going to give up that old relic and go for some advanced Vovokan technology?" Telisa asked him over her link.

"I already have. The attendant spheres."

One of his two spheres orbited by on cue.

"Kind of. I meant more in the way of an offensive weapon like your rifle."

"I can work in that direction. I'd prefer to understand it fully. We don't want to be any more dependent on Shiny than we already are." He glanced at the alien weapon on her back, then added, "And we want to be able to use our weapons safely."

"Is that a stab at my chain lightning gun?"

"Well, honestly, we don't know enough about it. Like, how does it target things? You can't safely shoot it in the direction of any friendlies because you don't know how to select your target signature, if the thing even has that functionality."

"Yeah. The gun is a bit crude. But effective."

"Anyway, what I was originally saying is, I can make parts myself without Shiny having to do the prayers for me."

"You can 'make parts yourself' by praying to an alien god machine? Ha. Priceless. If Shiny takes off now, can we even get off the planet?"

"Depends on whether or not he takes the *Clacker* with him."

"We need another team member so we can split up and still operate in pairs," Telisa said, changing the subject.

"Agreed. I'm working on it."

"I want in. We can't have you simply hiring a bunch of beautiful young women!" she joked.

"Can I have at least one more?"

Telisa snorted. Magnus smiled.

They came to the end of an open area of rough rock. Straight ahead, a thick stand of native plants rose from fractures in the ground. Magnus looked for other living things but didn't spot any dangers.

Telisa slowed. She obviously didn't like the idea of reducing their line of sight any more than he did. He remembered the clear snake creature and how hard it had been to spot.

Magnus interfaced with a guardian sphere and sent it ahead into the stand of plants. Telisa noticed it fly by, then did the same with one of her spheres.

"It looks like bamboo as it comes up from the breaches in the rocks, but those ridiculous…pom-poms of green stuff are almost comical," Telisa said.

"Yes, but I'm getting used to it slowly. And it's less comical now that I've seen the green worms they're made of."

The guardian spheres reached the robot remains ahead without incident. Telisa and Magnus recalled the spheres and waded into the stalks. They advanced another twenty meters.

"We're here," she said, looking every which way. "Ah, there it is."

The machine had been smashed. Its legs were splayed at an angle resembling a spider crushed under a boot. The red rock had been singed black in a couple of spots.

"Looks like it burned out after taking a big hit," Telisa said.

"This took a considerable amount of force. The scouts are made of durable stuff."

"Something added a bit of wear and tear," Telisa said. She looked around nervously. "What's that smell?"

Magnus knelt before the remains of the scout. The smell was strong. "It's the scout. Maybe that's some chemical from the Gorgalan parts." He retreated. "It could be toxic."

"It could be the smell of whatever killed it," Telisa pointed out.

"Possible. None of the other scouts saw anything unusual."

"Bad luck."

"I'm not so sure. A predator would have had to be very elusive to do this without being seen by any of the other scouts."

"Hah, well think about it. Stealthy predators get more food than clumsy loud ones."

"True enough," Magnus conceded, holding his weapon at the ready.

"Maybe it was partially transparent, like the red snake thing," Telisa said. "I think I'll call it a ribbon snake. That red part inside reminded me of a long red ribbon."

They walked out of the concealing stalks to a relatively open spot. Magnus sent her a search spiral.

"Let's do a quick patrol and see what we can see. I'd like to get a feel for the central ruins, anyway."

They set off, weapons at the ready. Telisa walked in parallel with Magnus about three meters to Telisa's left. A large structure became visible above the nearby stalks.

"So much for our spiral. The buildings are in the way," Telisa observed.

"Shiny, do you know of anything large enough to kill off one of our scouts?" Magnus transmitted, including Telisa in the channel.

The alien responded almost immediately. "Several possibilities. Large predators do exist on the surface."

"That might explain the grilles," Telisa said. "The natives had to move freely through their city without being in danger from predators."

"You call this moving freely?" Magnus said. "These things are practically part of the wall."

"Yes. I think I understand that now, though. It isn't freely movable for us. We must be more like their

53

predators. These creatures most likely moved through the grilles without opening them. Think about the shape required—wide and flat—they were pancake-flat creatures and they probably slid through these openings and moved over the walls and ceiling. Like flat caterpillars."

"Or blobs of formless flesh," Magnus said.

"Oh, now we're talking real horror VR material."

"Other high probability causes, culprits, explanations," added Shiny. "More Terrans detected, noted, found within ten kilometers your location."

"There are other people around here?" Telisa blurted.

"If you're trying to give us the best chance of success, you need to brief us more completely," Magnus growled.

"Yes. You could have mentioned that earlier, you know!" Telisa said with anger growing in her voice.

"Previously not detected, noted, found. Currently not detected, noted, found."

"Uhm. I think that means you detected some Terrans briefly? Now they're below your radar, so to speak. To figuratively speak," Telisa said.

"Recent knowledge, development, discovery. Unable to warn, tell, divulge at younger temporal stage."

"Now that was just obtuse. We like to say that as 'I just found out about it myself,'" Telisa said.

"I just found out about it myself," Shiny repeated in his buzzy voice. He mimicked her defensive tone. Telisa couldn't help but laugh. Even Magnus found his annoyance evaporating as Shiny copied Telisa's statement.

"How many of them? Where?" Magnus asked.

Shiny offered them a map feed. Magnus saw a map of the ancient Konuan city. He saw the locations of dozens of Terrans almost directly across the bulk of the city from his current position.

"That's a big expedition or a tiny colony," Magnus said.

"Uh oh. If it's a colony, maybe most of them died off," Cilreth said.

"What else can you tell us about them, Shiny?" asked Telisa.

"Armed. In hiding. Associated by hierarchy of command. Rarely pairing off to mate, suggesting sexually homogeneous group."

"You have a way with words, Shiny," Telisa said.

"Appreciated, agreed, accepted."

Telisa turned to Magnus and spoke quietly. "Why are there other people here? Could they be smugglers? UNSF?"

"Could be. Settlers might be the best guess. It's an open world. But a hierarchy does imply a military presence. Yet they haven't appeared to arrest or kill us."

"They may not have seen us yet. Maybe we should run."

"They couldn't have missed the *Clacker*. It's huge. Cilreth didn't mention any Vovokan cloaking."

"We didn't see any cities from orbit. Must only be a few of them, right?"

"I think so. We could send out a couple of scouts and see what we can see. I'd rather avoid them and continue our work on this side of the ruins. They may not be wanting any visitors."

Michael McCloskey

Chapter 6

Holtzclaw forced himself to look over the body of one of his soldiers. It lay broken across the red rocks at his feet. It was the same as always. Most of the flesh had been gouged or dissolved away from the shoulder blades upward. Only parts of the brain remained within the skull. The stench of ammonia lingered over the corpse. Holtzclaw did a mental accounting.

The forty-fourth victim of the monster. Assuming there really is only one.

Captain Arakaki believed strongly it was the work of only one Konuan. She had a lot of data to back the idea up. The pattern of kills, their distance apart, and the frequency of attacks all supported the idea that only one creature was out there killing them.

Or at least only one creature at a time. Maybe they take turns like some kind of hunting club.

Holtzclaw had Arakaki on the Konuan almost full time. She had the authority to pull a kill team whenever she chose. She had yet to do so, and Holtzclaw knew it was because she was a perfectionist. She wouldn't scramble the team until she knew they had a very real shot at slaying the creature.

Until then, it had the initiative. Their sensors weren't tracking it for the most part, though there were tantalizing clues, ghosts really, and half the time even those proved to be deceptions. Holtzclaw had no doubt about one thing: that creature was smart, smart on the level of full sentience. Maybe smarter than the Terrans.

A couple of soldiers wrapped the man up in blackvines. The dead had two destinations here: cremation or burial in one of the plant fissures. Most of the men chose cremation, but this man, Hummel, had been something of a nature lover and had chosen to be put into a fissure to become plant food. The soldiers carried him away.

Holtzclaw looked after the receding corpse and felt his morale slip one iota further into the void.

We're slowly dying here. Not just from the Konuan, but from everything. There can't really be any point in resisting the UNSF any longer, can there?

Sometimes Holtzclaw would discuss it with his officers. The new frontier was a big place. They wouldn't necessarily have to surrender. They could go out and join some of the outfits coming together far from Earth, and no one would come looking for them for a long time, if ever. Yet the dream of humanity freed from the old government of the core worlds was something they all believed in so strongly, they hadn't given up.

Holtzclaw thought about the recent landing again. Whoever it was, they had come in a big ship. They had to have a lot of supplies. Maybe even mobile factories that could produce new hardware with the right specs to feed into them. He had a feeling they had to turn this to their advantage or it might be over. They had to risk action now.

He used his link to call his officers in for a FTF. He told them to show up at the surveillance tent. It was close to Holtzclaw, in his sight at the moment. He headed for it at a slow walk, knowing the others would take longer to arrive. They had built their above-surface camp carefully, molding it to the terrain and the alien plant stalks to achieve concealment. They only needed access to one of the Trilisk tunnels, because the entire system was interconnected beneath the ruins. A system of active camouflage nets covered the entire camp, open space and all, so that men could walk between the tents and the underground entrance without notice from above.

Holtzclaw arrived at the surveillance tent, a long, low tent set to a green that matched the clumps of plant material above. He scratched fiercely at the growing skin on his shoulder, then ducked into the tent. Captain Caicedo sat inside among a large collection of stripped drones. The machines had been cannibalized for parts.

"Anything?"

"I don't think there's many of them, sir," Caicedo said, focusing his attention on some virtual display. Caicedo was a calm, strong officer. His expansive forehead displayed bulging arteries, even though his skin was dark. "But the ship is huge. There are robots crawling around that quarter of the city. Looks like about a dozen small scout robots. I'm thinking they're looking for something—same as us."

That idea bolstered Holtzclaw's resolve. If someone else was willing to expend a huge amount of resources to come here, then maybe, just maybe, there was something worth finding. Alien artifacts had turned the tide of the war once—against the UED—and finding more artifacts might turn the tide again. Or so the ragged band of soldiers hoped. But they had lost so many, and their ships were dwindling. It was a hope that diminished every day.

Holtzclaw waited for more officers. Major Kowalewski, Major Silvarre, Captain Arakaki, and First Lieutenant Racca walked in within two minutes. Holtzclaw took a peek outside.

"Where's Schimke?" he asked.

"I think he's too far into the tunnels," Racca offered. Holtzclaw shrugged and decided to start.

"We don't see that many of our guests. We can take that fat ship for ourselves," Holtzclaw declared.

"What if there's a lot more of them inside?"

"If it had been a drop ship filled with a battalion of space force marines or frontal assault robotics, we'd already be dying," Major Kowalewski said. "You can rule that one out."

"So if it's not a military ship, it has to be either a big settlement going down or a scientific expedition," said

Racca. "The fact they landed here at the edge of the Konuan city indicates the latter."

"Not necessarily. Settlers might make use of the shelter in the Konuan buildings or tunnels," Silvarre said.

Holtzclaw dismissed the idea. He shook his head. "If they came prepared, they have their own more advanced shelters in mind. It would only be a bunch of refugees, a group that was out on their luck, that would think like that."

This could be the best thing that could have happened to us, Holtzclaw thought. *If they're scientists in a ship that big, they have all the equipment we need to get the Trilisk machines and get out. One step closer to being able to fight the UNSF on even terms again.*

"No matter who they are, they have things we can use. And this planet is just hospitable enough they'll be able to survive even if we take some of the best for ourselves. We won't be sentencing them to death."

"Except by the monster," Arakaki said.

She's the only one who would say that, Holtzclaw thought, but he wasn't angry.

"They have to deal with the monster one way or another, now that they're here, same as we have. Unless you can kill it before we take off. In fact, they may have something we can use to finish it off."

Arakaki nodded. Holtzclaw wanted to try and use the Hellrakers on the thing, but given they could barely detect it, he didn't know if it would work, and he couldn't afford to use the supplies or the wear and tear on their smart artillery machines. Besides, most of the time if it appeared on their scans, it was because it was right on top of their camp.

Still...with a Hellraker it only takes one good shot. And we're about to that level of desperation.

"We should use the whole unit, show them how outnumbered they are in a fast strike, and force a quick surrender. No need to let this get bloody," Silvarre suggested.

"I agree, but I think the Hellraker is all the leverage we need," Holtzclaw said. "However, time is important here. We'll jam their communications and make our move. Take their equipment and use it to find what we want, then get out of here before any other ship could show up."

"Should we approach by ground or by air?"

"Ground, in case they have assets in orbit we don't know about," Racca said.

No one dissented. Holtzclaw agreed.

"T minus eighteen hours. Once we're set up to cover that entire side of the city, activate the jamming systems. I want them cut off from any other people they have in the system. Then we'll move in and seize their supplies."

"Yes, sir."

Michael McCloskey

Chapter 7

A nearby scout alerted Cilreth of the approach of her teammates. She stood amidst the chaos of a nascent camp. She had selected a reasonably flat, clear area nestled against an old Konuan building. The foam floor she had sprayed down was almost dry. With the help of her scout robots she had moved the containers from their sleeping spot to the new camp. Most of the equipment was better left in the containers until needed, but every container could be quickly accessed and wasn't part of the support for the tent. She addressed them through her link as Telisa and Magnus cleared the last stand of native plants.

"That was fast. I've got hours left to go," Cilreth said, though in truth the camp was perfectly workable already, though it had no well or solar array deployed.

I just enjoy setting stuff up in a new place.

Cargo containers had started to form a shelter around the perimeter, and she'd put up an all-weather fabric cover to the area. A scout robot showed up, carrying one of the last containers on its back. It looked like an ant carrying a squarish boulder.

"We don't know what killed the scout, but Shiny found people, Terrans I mean, on the other side of this old city."

"I can't reach Shiny," Cilreth said. "I was meaning to ask you about it."

Telisa was silent for a moment. "I don't know, but it can't be a good sign," she said.

"What?" Magnus said, lagging in the conversation. "Oh. I can't reach him either. Something is jamming us."

"Something…" Cilreth started.

"It must be the other humans," Telisa said. "They'd be the only ones who would know how to do that without examining our links."

63

"It is probably the Terrans, but of course, any advanced race could have detected the signals and decided to disrupt them," Magnus said. "Shiny could."

"You're still thinking he's against us?" Cilreth said.

Magnus shrugged. "That's not exactly what I meant, but still, it's possible he's doing it."

It's dangerous enough going to the frontier. We need to trust everyone on the team. Of course, I guess I quickly trusted Arlin and Leonard. Easier to trust my own race, I guess, justified or not.

"We can get along without him for now. The jamming could mean an imminent attack, though, down here or up there in orbit," Telisa said.

"It's worse than just losing touch with Shiny. I can only reach five scouts now," Magnus said.

"What will the others do?"

"They'll try and complete whatever mission each is on, then return to *Clacker*."

"Maybe we should return to the *Clacker*, too," Cilreth suggested.

"We need more information. I bet Shiny will figure out how to get back in touch with us. It's true he's not down here by our side, but he's a valuable asset up there."

"I'm going to go take a look at our Terran friends," Magnus said. "We can't make good decisions in the dark like this."

"Be careful," Telisa said.

Magnus looked thoughtful. "I know you've earned the stealth suit, but in this case it might be of more use to me. Just temporarily, of course," he said to Cilreth.

"I'd love to share," Cilreth said sweetly. "But no way is it going to fit your frame."

Magnus frowned. Telisa smiled.

"Don't be sad. I'm glad you're a large specimen, dear," she said playfully. "I have the stealthing sphere we picked up on Vovok, if you'd like to borrow it. And I do mean borrow! I can't go giving away all my superpowers."

Cilreth felt a bit of jealousy. *On a frontier expedition with your lover. Nice on the surface of it. Unless things go horribly wrong.*

Telisa tossed Magnus the tiny sphere from her pack. Somehow the Vovokan attendant spheres knew it was a peaceful transfer, so they didn't move to intercept.

Those things are amazing, Cilreth thought. *I need to figure out more about how they tick. Sigh. Later.*

"Thanks," Magnus said, slipping the sphere away in his pack. He headed off toward the center of the city. Telisa looked after him.

She's dependent on him. But I should cut her some slack; she just lost her father. Who else does she have? I think that was it.

Telisa hadn't mentioned a mother or other family, nor had Leonard.

"Well, at least it will go faster setting up the camp with two of us," Cilreth said. Telisa returned her attention to the campsite.

"The camp looks sleepable," Telisa said. "Let's go take a peek in those big buildings over there before nightfall. I promise I'll help with the camp more later."

"Without Magnus?"

"We're both armed," Telisa said. "And we have the scouts, at least the ones close by that can still hear us."

"When he gets back, if he finds us missing…"

"I'll leave a message here with the cargo containers. They can transfer it to his link when he gets within range. Besides, I bet Shiny's all over this jamming problem."

"He's certainly very capable. I'm still wrapping my head around having a giant centipede monster on my team."

"He's not a monster. Remember that," Telisa said.

Oops. Did I say that out loud? Cilreth frowned. The comment would have slid by with Magnus, but Telisa was avidly behind Shiny and trusted him completely.

Cilreth checked the scouts. "Magnus took one scout with him. Let's leave one to watch the camp and take three with us?"

"Sounds great," Telisa said. "I'll tell them not to wander far off. No use in losing more. We might gain one or two as we move."

They both drew their stunners as they moved out. Telisa caught sight of Cilreth's stunner and stopped.

"Hrm. Where are the weapons cases?" Telisa asked herself aloud.

Funny how people can be perfectly comfortable in a link conversation; then they speak to themselves out loud. Cilreth did the same thing sometimes. She thought maybe the habit formed when people were alone. They wanted to hear a voice, so they chatted to themselves aloud. So now she sometimes talked to herself inside her head, sometimes through her link, and sometimes out loud.

Telisa turned back. Cilreth didn't answer the question because she knew Telisa could use her link to ask the cases for anything she wanted.

Or has the jamming gotten worse?

As a test, Cilreth queried the inventory service of a nearby case. It sent queries out to the other cases and found the weapons containers for her. Telisa was already opening one of them. Cilreth scanned the nearby stalks for any signs of danger.

Telisa came back with a smart pistol in her hand. Cilreth had familiarized herself with the projectile weapons, though she preferred the stunner as a safer alternative. The weapon had a few smart rounds in it, capable of locking onto any target the user specified. The smart rounds could turn away or self-destruct in flight if they neared something that didn't fit the target profile.

However, on an alien planet, one would likely forego any target profiles since it was impossible to tell exactly what kind of dangerous animal you might come across.

Cilreth's link told her Telisa had put negative signatures into the weapon for the three Terrans, so it would be difficult (though not impossible) to accidentally shoot a friend.

"Better if we have radically different weapons by default," Telisa said. "In case something we find is immune to either one."

Cilreth nodded. She figured as much. Between the two of them and the scouts, they had a variety of weapons. She noticed the pistol had a new accessory attached to its underside.

"What's the new device?"

Telisa's eyebrows rose in a question; then she deduced what Cilreth was asking about.

"Oh. Under the barrel? It's a one-shot glue grenade."

"Nice. I'm not quite used to all the weapons yet. From private investigator to planetary explorer, you know."

"Isn't it wonderful?" Telisa asked enthusiastically.

Cilreth chuckled. *So young and full of energy.* "Which way are we going?"

Telisa was silent for a moment; then a scout robot headed out. "Follow him," she said.

They followed the robot out of the clearing. As they came to the first tight group of alien plants, Cilreth automatically reached for her machete.

"Shall I cut a swath through? Or do we want a low-profile trail behind us?"

"If there were no people, I'd say go ahead and cut. Predators will be equipped to find us anyway. But with people we don't know in the ruins, let's leave it."

Cilreth nodded. She agreed with the thinking. If she left a trail, it would make it easier for Magnus to follow if he needed to find them but also easier for strangers to find them.

"We have a box of breadcrumb devices we could use," Cilreth pointed out.

"Oh yeah. I never quite saw the usefulness of the devices before."

"They are usually just for marking a complex path for others to follow later after you're gone. Some places screw with a link's ability to accurately map them, and sometimes there isn't a way to send your map to the next person to come along."

"And we can configure them to be silent when strangers come by," Telisa noted. She was probably reading up on them in her link to remind herself of their capabilities.

"But in this case, I'm wondering if we can form a bridge with them. If they can each reach twenty five meters or so, then we could daisy chain our communications back here."

"Daisy chain?" There was a delay. Then Telisa nodded. "Okay. But I hope we stop coming up with new plans every five minutes, or we'll never get anything done!"

Young people. Every time I use an archaic term they have to look it up. "Ha." Cilreth ran back and retrieved a pack of fifty breadcrumbs. Each device was a small black cylinder, the size of five or six tiny coins stacked together. She configured them as a relay chain and told them to only offer services to the three Terrans or Shiny. Then she jogged back to Telisa and dropped the first one at the entrance of the plant cluster.

"There we go," Cilreth said.

Telisa pushed aside the green masses of moss-like leaves and stepped through. Her spheres slipped through after her, dodging around swaying green mops and thick stalks. Cilreth followed.

They had walked about a hundred meters from camp when the scout stopped. Cilreth immediately stopped with it, staring ahead. She had just dropped a third breadcrumb device behind her. She accessed the scout's view. Its Vovokan mass detectors had sensed movement ahead, over and above the normal flutter of the green plant bulbs in a light breeze. She checked the mass map. The movement was fifteen meters ahead, and slightly underground.

A trap? Thank Cthulhu for those scout machines.

"There," Telisa said through her link, sending Cilreth a visual indicator. Telisa pointed out a hole in the ground under a batch of stalks. One of the natural plant pot wells. Cilreth was able to confirm the movement came from inside the well.

Cilreth stayed put and watched. Nothing much seemed to be happening on the surface. She watched until she thought maybe Telisa would just keep going. Then she spotted something moving. This time she was ready to interpret what she saw: another translucent creature.

It was small. Then she saw another. More tiny clear creatures climbed out from the plant well. They scampered over the spiky red rock.

"Critters. Just some clear critters, like ghost shrimp," Cilreth transmitted. For some reason they reminded her of ghost shrimp in size and movement, though she could not tell if they had legs or not.

"The last small critters I found tried to eat me alive," Telisa said. She had her pistol pointed in their direction. Cilreth knew the grenade launcher was probably being armed to the signature of those clear creatures.

"You're not going to shoot first, are you?" she asked a bit nervously.

"No way," Telisa said. "I'm not looking for trouble. Let's just skirt around." But she did not move.

"Watch the plants for the red snake things, too," Cilreth said. "Where there's prey…"

"Good point," Telisa agreed. She lowered her pistol.

Cilreth spotted one of the creatures pulling a piece of plant along the rock. Then it fell back into the black hole of the well carrying the debris.

"They're carrying stuff that fell into the plant well," Cilreth pointed out. "That's why there's no detritus lying around. They carry it in there, and it must be for food."

"Or to grow food with," Telisa added.

"You don't think…they couldn't be intelligent, could they?"

"I doubt it," Telisa said slowly.

"It's just that they could fit through the grilles."

Telisa stopped. She had to be thinking about it. "Yeah, but why are they living in a hole in the ground when they could live in the buildings?"

"Hrm. Yeah. I'm sure they're not smart. Just trying not to make any assumptions."

They sped up as the clear colony of harvesters was left in the rear. Cilreth kept placing the trail-marking devices as they went. Within another ten minutes, their scout leader arrived at a cluster of Konuan buildings.

Cilreth pinged their camp through the chain of breadcrumb devices. Everything appeared to be working. She took stock of the structures. They looked similar to what they'd already seen, only taller and denser.

Cilreth checked her link for Shiny and Magnus. She still couldn't get any response, even through the chain back to camp.

"Any reason you like these?" she asked Telisa, referring to the buildings.

"Yes. They're situated over a system of underground chambers and tunnels. It kinda reminds me of what we found on Thespera. I'm hoping the tunnels below were used or built by Trilisks."

Telisa selected one of the five grilles that dotted their side of the nearest building. A scout started to pick away at the setting around the grille. Telisa made a frustrated sound. Cilreth took a look. She thought it might take the scout about ten minutes to dig into the building.

"I'm going to send a scout to our ship. Shiny gave me some kind of digging device; I still have it around," Telisa said. "I don't think it's at the camp."

"Really? Were the walls made of tough stone on Vovok?" asked Cilreth.

"I'm not sure how hard they were. Besides, it was the Trilisk trap. Thespera, not Vovok. But the item is workable enough."

"That would be cool. These bars are rugged, though. They were built to last. Impressive for a primitive race, actually."

"Well, even if it doesn't work on the grilles, the robots get through eventually."

"I assume the walls are usually even stronger."

"Maybe. I could think of a reason why not, though. If the Konuan used them to keep predators out of their dwellings, then it would be enough to look like this was the only hole through. The predator might try to dig there. Especially if it saw or smelled a Konuan flit through there. But the predator might not try to break through what looks like a rocky mountainside."

Cilreth shrugged. "Fair enough. Whatever works for us to get around. Otherwise, I'm gonna get a pickaxe and end up with arms like Jaggor."

"Who?"

"Oh. Never mind. I'm showing my age."

Telisa nodded. If her link hadn't been jammed, it might have told her about the old VR called *Jaggor the Hunter-Gatherer*. The daisy chain reference was probably in her dictionary cache. The information was most likely available in the huge data cache of the *Clacker* orbiting above. Cilreth was just as happy to leave the reference unexplained.

Finally the scout shifted the loosened grill in the wall. Telisa and Cilreth stepped forward and helped to break it free. Then Telisa took her pistol out again and sent a scout in.

The machine's lights gave them a preview of the room. It looked similar to the ones they had already seen, though more cluttered. Rusted metal implements hung from racks on four walls.

"An old armory? Those could be weapons," Cilreth said.

"Hrm. Maybe," Telisa said. "If a blob of protoplasm can hold a sword. They fit through the grilles, of course. You know what? It must have been hard to carry anything large around in those dwellings."

"Oh yeah, major limitation. That shows how important those grilles are to them. If your theory about predators is the explanation, there must have been a constant threat from them."

"Yet the Trilisks come here and add the tunnels below. We need to figure out why the Trilisks came here. What are they doing on these planets? Research on alien life? Conquest?"

Cilreth smiled. *It would be nice to know, but they're gone now. I'm more interested in their toys and how they can improve our lives.* "So how many more grilles to get to the nearest tunnel?"

"Probably four or five more," Telisa said.

"If the grilles are for predators, you'd expect them to be sufficient on outside-facing entrances only."

Telisa turned back toward the entrance. "Ah. The scout has come back." Cilreth followed her gaze. Another scout scrambled into the room. Telisa plucked a tool from its back.

The device was a long stack of red cubes held in a silver frame. One end was broad and flat.

"That thing looks so weird! I guess given how odd Shiny looks, I shouldn't be surprised his tools look radical, too."

Telisa pointed the flat end of the machine at the wall beside a grille and activated it. It made a gentle humming noise. Cilreth felt air moving through the room. "Whoa." She looked around.

"It's this thing," Telisa said. "Sorry, I should have mentioned it makes a whirring sound and the air moves around a lot when I use it."

Telisa started again. Cilreth watched the stone around the side of the grille disappear. Then she saw a pile of gray liquid forming under the device.

"Yech," she said. "It's digging so fast!"

Telisa smiled. "We need one of these on every scout," she said. "Magnus will be happy. I bet Shiny can make us more of these."

"If we can get a hold of him again. I know, he's probably working on it."

The grille was removed in record time. A scout machine slipped into the next room. Bright reflections of silvery metal shone in the machine's lights.

"Wow, something interesting in there," Telisa said.

Cilreth took a peek. She thought it looked like a giant spider's web of silver fibers. "Is it safe?"

"What makes you ask now?"

If I say it looks like a spider web, it'll sound dumb. "Sorry, just an instinctual reaction to what looks like a giant spider web. But maybe we should know what's up before going in there?"

Telisa didn't say anything. But she walked a second scout machine in and had it look around with the other one.

"The web things are modular," Telisa noted. "Each one is a network of filaments, roughly two meters square, with twelve little silver discs woven into it."

Cilreth watched the scout machine feeds as one of the scouts touched a web with the tip of a leg. Nothing seemed to happen. The network was bright like new, but it wasn't sticky. Nothing moved.

"Okay, I'm heading in there. I'd like to take one of these back for further study," she said.

Telisa went in and started to collect one of the webs. Cilreth knelt down and waddled through after her.

Cilreth got a closer look at the room. Each shiny webbing had been made from filaments of silver metal. Dispersed along the web every ten centimeters or so, thick discs the size of a palm were woven into the network. The webs hung from old metal hangers built into the walls and ceiling. A few lay on the floor.

"They've been arranged in here," Cilreth said. "It's just a storage room."

"Seems like it, doesn't it? The webs could easily fit through the grilles, so they weren't necessarily made in here." Telisa finished folding it up and put it into a black sample bag.

"I don't have a lot of theories about these things," Cilreth said. "But next door there were weapons. So I'm thinking these could be weapons, too."

"One thing is odd…these discs here are batteries. Advanced batteries. They're beyond anything we've seen in the Konuan ruins so far."

"Trilisk, then?" asked Cilreth.

"No. Too primitive."

"Then maybe the outlying Konuan were primitive slaves to the high-tech city Konuan."

"I'm thinking the Trilisks were advancing them, showing them how to improve themselves," Telisa said.

"Really? Interesting. I can easily pose a more sinister theory: the Trilisks took over, and the few traitor Konuan who served them got cool toys to keep the other Konuan in line."

"You are so cynical. It's possible, though," Telisa said.

Cynical is my middle name. "Didn't you experience a Trilisk memory? I take it you saw into the mind of one, and it was a nice creature? You felt it wanted to help?"

"Well, not really. It was angry at other aliens that had attacked its world at the time and wanted revenge. Not exactly a loving moment. I think it was ruthless to its enemies."

"Well, sounds like they may have been mean creatures," Cilreth said.

"Maybe, but like I said…the aliens had just killed a bunch of Trilisks, I think. I would be angry, too. The memory is just at a bad moment for measuring their overall disposition."

I bet I could tell if I had experienced it, Cilreth thought. *If you could be in someone else's head for just thirty seconds, couldn't you tell?*

The more Cilreth thought it over, the less certain she became of her initial reaction. If you read the mind of a murderer when she was thinking about her favorite restaurant, could you really pick up the killer vibe? Probably not.

They checked the grilles in each direction, looking for something interesting. Cilreth checked the grille on her left. A complicated shape lay in the darkness.

"Over here," she said.

Telisa lit the scene with her powerful flashlight. A scout added to the illumination with its own lights.

"Whoa, that's no primitive anything," Cilreth said.

The shape was a robot. It had an upright, rocket-shaped body with a tripedal base. Its three legs were staggered at sixty degrees from its three arms. The base of the body rested against the floor. Its smooth sapphire exterior glittered in the light. From beyond the grille the upright body looked thicker than a Terran.

Almost as an afterthought, Telisa broke out of her fascinated stare and grabbed the breaker claw from her belt. Cilreth saw the move and followed her lead, drawing her stunner. Then she frowned, replaced the stunner, and took out her machete. Telisa gave her a questioning look. Cilreth shrugged.

"Maybe it's an alien death machine so advanced the designers never thought 'what if someone tries to hack its legs off?'" she said defensively. Then she asked, "What kind of robot is it?"

"I've never seen anything like it," Telisa said. "But its trilateral symmetry suggests…"

"Trilisks?"

Telisa said nothing, as if uttering the possibility would nix her rising hopes.

"Three legs, though?" Cilreth persisted. "How does it walk? Or, how *did* it walk?"

"Well, just look at them. They're jointed funny."

"Okay, I guess nature can make almost anything work," Cilreth said.

"Think of the primitive Konuan. If they were around when this thing was operational, they must have been terrified. It would have been like a rock god to them."

"The Trilisks may well have been here playing god," Cilreth said. "Them and their prayer machines, producing things out of thin air."

Telisa paused and opened her pack.

"What do you need?" Cilreth asked.

"I'm making sure we don't have an active AI nearby that can produce things for us," Telisa said. She finished looking through her back. "No candy bars. Their machines must be inoperative, like this robot."

Cilreth laughed. "We're developing a checklist for exploration. Land on a new planet, step one, see if prayer works."

"Help me get this thing onto a scout. I don't want to be dragging it all the way back."

"Yes, I'm sure we can, but they can barely fit in and out of here as it is. A scout will have to drag it."

Telisa swore. "You're right, of course. It must have come from below." Telisa pointed out a circular portal in the floor where the Konuan grille would usually lie.

Telisa and Cilreth worked to attach the derelict machine to one of the scouts. Cilreth wished she had one of the cargo case lids to use as a sled, but those were far behind them. They finally decided an alien robot skin was probably durable enough to survive dragging until they could make a sled from plant stalks outside.

"Its perfect blue surface is creepy. I feel like I'm looking into a lake when I stare at it. What if it sucks the juice from the scout and comes back to life?" Cilreth said.

"Shut up," Telisa said.

"What? It's not *that* crazy," Cilreth said.

"I know. You're scaring the crap out of me," Telisa said. "What choice do we have? I want that robot."

Cilreth nodded. *I guess I'm being too cynical. Even for me.* "Should we send it back now?"

Telisa scratched her chin then nodded. "What good would it be in a fight now? Its weapon mount is blocked." She laughed. "How are we going to break that one to Magnus? A definite design flaw. Scouts carrying cargo can't really fight."

Cilreth smiled. "Room for improvement in version three. I think we have enough to head back to the *Clacker* now."

"Yes. I just want to verify we're over a Trilisk tunnel here."

"This robot isn't enough?"

77

The scout machine carrying the robot headed back. Then another scout attached a smart line and dropped down the hole like a giant spider. Its sensory feed showed a dusty tunnel below.

"It's something very different than this building. I want to take a quick peek," Telisa said.

Oh man. We'll never get back at this rate.

Telisa dropped down and made an appreciative noise. Cilreth kept watching the views from below through a scout robot.

"These are much more advanced than the ruins above," Cilreth said.

Telisa just stared at the walls and a nearby column.

"Did you hear me?" Cilreth asked over her link.

Telisa turned to look up at Cilreth and spoke in an excited whisper. "Cilreth, I think this area was constructed by the Trilisks just as Shiny suspected."

"I—" Cilreth began; then she heard a scrabbling sound behind her. "Something's up here!"

Chapter 8

Captain Arakaki made her way along the ridge toward the tunnels where the settlers hid themselves.

Of course, she had been watching them for months. One of their sensor probes sat on a nearby rocky cliff overlooking the ridge. Holtzclaw had interviewed them back when they first arrived on the planet. He told Arakaki it was a sad collection of men from some doomed expedition or settlement. He had told her the survivors were so traumatized by being hunted by the Konuan that they had started to worship it as some kind of god of death.

Arakaki rolled her eyes as she recalled hearing about it.

My race loves to escape reality through self-deception.

Holtzclaw said the men lived simple lives, eating sugar from some photosynthesis modules and the roots of a few Terran plants they managed to get growing. Arakaki knew a lot about them, but there was one thing she didn't know. Why had the Konuan failed to kill the last few of them off? She intended to find out.

Arakaki idly chewed on a cigarette-sized strip of some tough synthetic. It was all that was left of her ex—a man literally blown to bits—and though it seemed odd, chewing on that surviving piece of his battle exoskeleton was her way of remembering him. That, and she always had to be chomping on something anyway or else she felt incomplete.

She saw one of the trees on the ridge was shedding. Its thousands of component worms were writhing along the red rocks, seeking other stalk holes. Every now and then one of the trees just did that. Some UED scientist had said it was the end of the life cycle: the tree dissolved into a thousand green worms that spread its genetic material to other stalk plants among dozens of nearby fissures in the rock. A week later the Konuan had killed him.

Some of the worms might make it a hundred meters, though the little clear shrimp things in the holes liked to scamper out and eat them. Arakaki thought it was all kind of gross, but she had seen a lot worse, even in the food courts at Terran starports.

She stopped to take an extra look. Where the green crawlies migrated, there were the shrimp-like feeders, which meant cleargliders. Did that also mean the event might attract even bigger predators in turn? The vicinity looked clear to her and her weapon's sensors.

Finally Arakaki ignored the green caterpillars and sidled up to the opening in the rock where the settlers had been found. Her weapon detected signatures of four men just inside the entrance. She paused, listening, then slipped inside.

One of the men, bald, in a yellow robe, carefully cut up some kind of plant root. Another, also in a yellow robe but with short, light-colored hair, worked on a handheld device she didn't recognize. The other two men looked similar, with reddish robes. They sat on the floor with their eyes closed, either meditating or accessing their PVs.

"Don't move suddenly or I'll blow your asses off," she summarized.

All four men started at her sudden statement. Arakaki watched carefully. Though they all moved in response before their minds could fully process the meaning of her threat, none of them reached for any weapons, so they lived.

"Please don't fire," one of the men said. He had a ruddy nose and star-baked skin that almost matched his red robes.

"Surprise inspection," Arakaki barked, as if that were all the explanation necessary. Arakaki kept her weapon in the general direction of the acolytes. With their signatures logged, it would require minimal aiming to wipe them all out with a single mental command or pull of her finger.

"Where are your supplies?" she asked.

"We don't have anything of use to you," another one said. The one who had answered had no hair. He wore a plain yellow robe.

"Show me what you have. I want to know how you survive out here."

"In here," said the bald man in the yellow robe.

Arakaki chomped down on the sliver in her mouth and followed. Her finger was relaxed near the trigger of her PAW, and her thoughts remained close to the fire control in her link.

They led her to another dismal rock room. She carefully squatted and followed them through a pulled Konuan grille. More grilles were still in place above and below, but the grilles in the other four directions had been pulled out.

"Here are many of our supplies," the man said. "Of course, we have some equipment deployed around. Solar cells and some photosynthesis modules are over our heads, on the top of the ridge."

The man indicated a waist-high pile of packs and equipment. Arakaki looked things over, still keeping one eye on the pilgrims.

She found a PSG stunner, three grenades, and two large projectile weapons. She saw clips for some other handheld projectile weapons. There were food wrappers and some half-empty backpacks. She counted eight of the backpacks.

"Where did you get that stuff?"

"That's what little we have left of our equipment."

A metal sphere attracted her attention. At first she thought it was a grenade, but it was too large. She reached out to pick it up. As her hand approached, a small handle extended for her to grasp. It was lighter than a grenade.

So it has power…but it doesn't offer my link any services. So what the hell is it? "What's this?" Arakaki demanded.

"I don't know," the man said.

She put it within her pack without taking her attention from her weapon. "I saw your packs in the other room. These aren't yours. Those weapons are varied. Also not yours. Some of them are new. Obtained since Holtzclaw interviewed you before."

"The UED leader? I thought he decided to leave us alone. We've had various members join us from all over the frontier. No deserters from the UED, though."

"Then where are they? Answer my questions or else. We've tolerated you for a long time. You don't want to be on our bad side. You know we have artillery covering this site. We can send a present your way anytime we want."

"We've lost some pilgrims. The planet can be cruel. Also, some strangers came by from time to time. They were violent. It wasn't our intention. But we have to defend ourselves."

"You men? You keep the pistols under your robes?"

The men were silent for a moment. "Yes, we have pistols. But usually we let the Konuan handle troublemakers."

Troublemakers…like me. Like the UED soldiers who have died?

She made a point of aligning her weapon at the head of the man who spoke. "You're on its side, then," she said. "You help it kill us."

"Only the ones who come in here and threaten us directly. Please just leave."

"The Konuan protected us," another said.

Another of the men winced as he said it.

That must be true. Or is he wincing because he knows that guy's a buckle bulb?

"You confuse protection with predation," she said. "Why hasn't it eaten you?"

"We respect it. We learn from it."

"It is smart," Arakaki said. "Real smart. But why would it teach you anything?"

"If you want to see it, we can show you."

Arakaki's face tightened. "What do you mean, show me?"

"The Konuan. We can show you. You can meet it. See for yourself. Leave your weapons, pledge yourself to it, and it will spare you."

"Like it spared the owner of that stunner there? Or the owner of that sugar kit?"

"They didn't give up their weapons. They were a threat. It easily dispatched them."

"Finally, something I believe. Okay, show me where I can meet it, then take off."

"If you try to harm it—"

"I'll take my chances. Now hurry up," Arakaki said.

The bald man in the robe nodded assent and walked off. Arakaki stepped away from the others, then turned to follow.

The man led her through a patch of blackvines. Arakaki scanned the sluggishly moving tendrils of the plants for concealed danger. Her eyes and her weapon didn't note anything amiss.

Beyond the blackvines, they came to a dirty old tunnel. *This could be Trilisk*, Arakaki thought. *But this isn't very deep.*

She knew that under the square chambers of the Konuan, which were stacked atop each other haphazardly, the Trilisk tunnels ran from building to building. The UED soldiers had not figured out why the Trilisks had built the tunnels, though some thought it was to spy on the Konuan or conduct experiments on them without being seen.

Arakaki smelled the monster.

This guy knows what he's talking about. The monster has been here. No doubt they've been sacrificing people to it all along. That's why it left them alive. Until there are no people left.

They came to a large square room. It was a dead end at the moment, with its grilles intact.

It can still attack from any direction, and it can run if it senses an ambush. If the monster ever runs from anything.

A huge bowl in the center of the room held some bones.

What's left of the sacrifices.

The robed man turned to regard Arakaki. She pointed her carbine at his face. "Maybe I'll shoot your legs and leave you as the sacrifice this time," she said.

"It won't eat me. But it will eat you, if you insist on the weapons," he said.

She made a face of disgust and indicated the exit with a twitch of her barrel. "Beat it."

"What?"

"Take off. Now. Before I change my mind."

The man frowned, but he moved to the exit.

To him, I'm just another victim to his god. We'll see about that.

As soon as the pilgrim had left the room, Arakaki took out three grenades. She dropped two to the floor; the devices slowly rolled out to the left and right. They rolled through the grilles to take up positions in adjacent rooms.

She tossed the last grenade up through the grille on the ceiling. That was the direction of attack she feared the most: it liked to dissolve Terrans' heads off.

The grenades armed with a signature Arakaki had designed to try to match the Konuan. What few glimpses of the creature they had collected showed it was large, flat, and silent. It liked to move on walls and ceilings or across the plants just as often as it would be on the ground. It had a low body temperature despite being able to move very quickly. It was also associated with electromagnetic anomalies, but Arakaki had just used that to make the grenades even more likely to target and strike movement when odd fields were detected.

Arakaki leaned back against the cool wall beside the entrance tunnel. She touched the grenade around her neck. Ironically, its cold, deadly presence settled her nerves. She believed if that grenade ever went off, at least she would be taking the Konuan with her. She chomped on the sliver in her mouth.

With the grenade right around my neck, it'll be "a bang loud enough to wake Cthulhu up." That's what he used to say about the Hellrakers.

She drew her laser pistol with her left hand, then waited.

Within ten minutes she got a ping. The UED sensor stationed on a nearby cliffside had picked something up. Arakaki had been tuning their probes to detect the Konuan for a long time. Though the probe's mission had been to detect Terrans and Terran machines, the probes had a wide range of sensory abilities. This probe told her now that something was approaching, and it wasn't human.

Arakaki felt a rush hit her system. She wanted to do something, to shoot or break into a sprint, anything. But she just took a deep breath and waited.

The contact slipped away for a few seconds, then came back, closer to the caves where she waited. Then it moved still closer.

Will it come in behind me or drop in from above?

The contact moved within an eighth of a kilometer, then disappeared.

It's in the tunnels ahead of me, she guessed. Arakaki slowed her breathing and watched her weapon's sensors. Nothing. The grenades hadn't seen anything, either.

Another minute scraped by. Arakaki heard something, distant, so faint she wasn't sure if there had even been a noise. Another minute passed. The laser became heavy in her grasp. She leaned forward from the wall, standing with her weight even on each foot.

The probe outside picked the contact back up. It was moving away.

"Why won't you just die?" she whispered.

The ghost moved about a quarter of a kilometer, dropping in and out of sight. Then it stopped. It didn't leave the range of the probe. It lingered.

The damn thing wants me to come after it. So it can kill me somewhere else.

Arakaki almost growled in frustration. Then she opened a link to Holtzclaw.

"This is Captain Arakaki, requesting a Hellraker round," she said. Holtzclaw replied within three seconds.

"You'll have it in thirty seconds. Send the coordinates."

The ghost started to move away again.

"Frag me," she said aloud. "Scratch that," she added. "Sorry, sir."

She called back her grenades and snatched them up. Arakaki headed out after the sensor ghost.

Chapter 9

Magnus trailed his scout by ten meters through clumps of vegetation. He deployed his Veer suit's head guard 50 percent with a link command, just to add protection to the back of his head. He nudged aside plant stalks with his rifle. More and more, he found himself squatting to take a peek under the greenish clumps growing on the alien foliage. From a position near the ground, he could see much farther, but it was pretty uncomfortable to crawl along for any distance.

He felt a bit sluggish. Shipboard training had gone well with all the extra space on the *Clacker*, but he may have overdone it. He still wasn't used to Vovokan ships or equipment. The VR facilities were amazing. And the quasi-virtual training machines he'd prayed up with Shiny's help were top-notch as well. He only regretted that their team was so small. With the *Clacker*, he felt like he could train an entire company.

I don't even want to run Parker Interstellar Travels. What would I do with more people? I guess I would train some great teammates like Telisa and hit the dirt on more unexplored planets.

Ever since the UNSF had trained Magnus to "hit the dirt" on planetary assaults, he had been hooked on it. Now that he was a free agent, it was easier than going in after the assault machines and cleaning up. They just dropped on whatever alien ruins they felt curious about and poked around.

He skirted the largest ruins at the center of the city, making his way around them on the northern side. The plants were numerous, even in the city. The way they grew from the round fissures in the rocks made them look like they'd been there for a long time. Maybe they had been part of the city at its peak. But he knew that conclusion was suspect: Who knew how these alien plants worked?

Maybe they somehow drilled their own holes in the rock wherever a seed fell. If they even had seeds. Thinking of seeds made him remember the green worms: maybe that was how the plant spread. Its "runners" really did run. Or squirm.

They could just as easily dig their way up from underground, he mused.

Up ahead, he came into contact with another scout unit headed back. The scout had turned back toward the *Clacker* once the jamming started. He turned it around and added it to his team. He checked the machine's logs. It hadn't encountered any humans, though it had seen one of the clear snakelike creatures hiding among the stalks.

Those things might be dangerous, even though my Vovokan spheres protected me once.

He stopped after half an hour and asked the forward scout to do a passive scan. For five minutes Magnus waited, crouched beside the ruin of a single-room building the size of a tiny hovel. He had plenty of time to look it over. The structure looked old. It had grilles on each face. The bars on the grilles were of a different design: they were made from the plant stalks.

Like wood, he thought. *But all the others we've seen are tough stone or ceramic. So this guy must have been poor. Or this building just predates the others.*

Magnus took a peek inside with a light. As he expected, a grille was in the center of the ceiling. There wasn't one on the floor. The walls and floor were littered with brown and green refuse that looked like rotted furniture or tools. Some short sticks came out of the walls and ceiling, but nothing else remained intact.

Magnus walked around the building to check out the far side. Two large plants grew from breaches in the rock next to the building. He saw something new there: grilles across the openings where the plants emerged from the ground. The stalks of the plants grew through the holes.

The grilles matched those of the building, made from pieces of cured or painted plant stalks.

That means they went down there. Telisa will be interested. Maybe they lived in those natural plant pots before they made their own structures. Like ancient Terrans living in caves.

A small gray critter of some kind darted inside. Magnus pointed his weapon. Thoughts of the vermin that attacked him on Vovok came to the fore. He took a deep breath and mastered the nervousness it brought.

On second thought, maybe it's a kind of animal pen to them. Those critters that live down there might have been raised like domestic animals. But they can get out. Which means the pen is to keep the predators out.

The results of the passive scan came back. Magnus opened a pane in his PV to look over the results. The information unfolded in his mind, and he instantly saw signs of scanning coming from a nearby hill overlooking the ruins. Someone had placed sensors there to keep track of what was going on in this area of the ruins.

So. We're curious about them, and of course, they're curious about us. Or they're just cautious.

Magnus examined the scan patterns more closely. The sources must be Terran, he decided. There was something familiar about them. He became apprehensive.

Military.

Magnus realized he was already in a lot of danger just being within the scan arc of the sensor he'd noticed. There was a good chance he hadn't been picked up, being a lone man in a Veer suit with a couple of small robots. His Veer suit masked his signature to some degree, at least at long distance. Of course, military sensors would be designed to defeat such obfuscation, since soldiers so typically wore them.

Magnus immediately moved to the side of the old building away from the source of the scans. He thought for

Michael McCloskey

a moment, then decided to continue. He sent a scout ahead
to find a route with some cover from the hill. The next
structure was not far. Magnus dropped low and moved
slowly to get behind the next building. And the next. He
stayed calm and alert. His link had the stealth device ready,
but he didn't want to use it unless he had to, since he
didn't know what its lifespan was.

*If something bad happens, hopefully I'll have enough
warning to activate it.*

His lead scout had come to the edge of a shallow
escarpment. Its video feed showed a small valley below its
position.

Magnus kept low. He decided to stay away from the
open area and rely on the scout's vision. The open valley
would mean danger of being spotted. He dropped to the
ground. The rocks were rugged and sharp, but the Veer
suit was more than enough protection.

Magnus accessed a binocular feed from the scout in
his PV, so he could get a three-dimensional view from the
machine. When he closed his eyes and concentrated, it was
as good as being there himself. He watched for a couple
minutes before he decided something looked wrong down
below. He activated an optic enhancement suite on the
scout to get the best possible look.

Magnus's breath caught in his throat. In one moment it
hit him hard: that was a camo net system. A Terran active
camo net.

Down below, he saw them. Men dressed in dark gray
fatigues. One of them wore a battle suit very much like his
own Veer skinsuit. The suit had adapted itself to the terrain,
taking on a light rust coloration.

Oh no.

Magnus shook his head as if to clear it. *UED soldiers?
Have I finally gone nuts?*

90

He took another look. They were still there. Magnus refused to believe for another moment. *Maybe I breathed in some hallucinogenic toxin. I'm just seeing things.*

He tried to contact Shiny.

There was no answer.

Magnus took one last look at the men below. They were grabbing gear. *Preparing to move out. Have they detected me?*

Magnus got up onto all fours to crawl away. His trailing scout became the lead, and he told them to slowly move back toward the *Clacker*.

The crack of a large projectile weapon thundered across the landscape. The scout at the edge of the escarpment behind him exploded into a thousand tiny fragments. A dozen of the bite-size pieces landed all around him.

Magnus dropped prone again. *Time for some serious cloaking!*

He activated the alien stealth field through his link. A moment later his other scout was vaporized.

Boooom.

Magnus decided to trust his cloaking. He stood and sprinted back the way he had come. From an open spot in the vegetation, he glanced southward. An assault machine walked toward him from a half kilometer away. It stood three meters tall, with four arms and four legs. It moved with a clumsier gait than that of his smaller scouts, though it was more intimidating. Each arm of the machine held weapons trained in his direction.

Magnus ran. He took long strides over the red rock, hopping here and there to cross sharp spots. Though he had activated the cloaking sphere, he could still see himself normally.

After half a minute he slowed down. The cloak seemed to be working, since he didn't detect any more fire incoming. He retraced his steps by the various buildings along the north side of the ruins. After he had traveled over a kilometer from the encounter, he slowed further.

Magnus returned to careful thought. His situation was like a virtual nightmare scenario. Yet it had to be real.

It's not as crazy as it feels. Parts of the UED had to have escaped. I guess I just thought they would have disbanded by now. But this is the frontier: rife with gangs and rogue corporations. It would be better to stay in a big, heavily armed group and find new means of sustenance.

Magnus had never had a flashback, but now he thought he must know what one felt like. Seeing those uniforms again after all this time brought it back. Most of the men in those dark gray uniforms and military skinsuits he had seen in the war had been dead, killed by space force assault robots. They had taken a few survivors prisoner here and there for mind probe specialists to interrogate. Magnus had done his part, though now he thought maybe he had been young and stupid to follow the orders. Maybe the men and women of United Earth Defiance had been on the better side. If he had it to do over again...

Magnus chafed at the lack of communications. The UED force was jamming them. It had to be it: they wouldn't want anyone reporting their presence to the space force. The *Clacker* must have scared the shit out of them. But now they were moving out, which meant they were coming to silence the explorers.

We have to cut our losses and get the hell off this planet.

He retreated quickly back the way he had come. The battle machine must not have been able to follow him, since he heard no more loud retorts from projectile launches. He knew such a machine had to be able to outpace a man, at least on clear terrain. The question was, would they rapidly reacquire him if the cloak ran out of power?

After an hour of moving through the ruins, Magnus realized something had gone wrong. Nothing looked familiar. At first he had thought he was only a bit off his previous course, and the many buildings did start to look the same after a while. But his intuition told him he had not come this way before.

I'm off course. I don't...ah. The cloak.

Somehow the cloaking device must have confused his link's mapper. The device was supposed to work through a combination of compass, accelerometer, and even incorporate the things Magnus saw. Normally it could even ping base camp or a ship in orbit for verification. But the first two, at least, must have interacted poorly with the alien cloaker. And the last one would be impossible due to the jamming. He had heard of stranger things happening. But the key now was what to do about it. Presumably he could deactivate the cloak, at least long enough to let his link get its bearings.

Magnus hid in a caved-in Konuan ruin and deactivated the cloak. He tried to contact Shiny again, but there was no response. His compass reading showed he had been moving north. He made a note of the correct direction, which now would be southeast instead of just east. Taking a rough guess at where he really was, Magnus told his link where he wanted to go. If he left the cloak off, maybe it could get him there.

Damn! A huge waste of time when we can't afford it.

The shadows within the hovel deepened. Night was coming.

Decision time. Can I make it in the dark? Do I want to try?

When Magnus remembered that the UED soldiers were moving out, it helped him make up his mind. If they were after the *Clacker*, then he had to get back first.

Though if they had swift means of transport, then they've already arrived while I was wandering around the ruins like an idiot.

Magnus left the old Konuan building as the star's light failed, and decided to find out what Chigran Callnir Four was like after dark.

Chapter 10

"What?" Telisa sent to Cilreth. The tone of her last message had been alarming. There was no reply.

Telisa grabbed the rope ascender in one hand and held her pistol in the other. The smart rope wrapped around her foot to lift her back up. Telisa heard something clack and scrape up above.

"Cilreth!" Telisa transmitted. There was no answer.

Sounds of a fight came from above. Telisa heard the thwump of a glue grenade launching.

Dammit! And we sent one of the scouts back!

Telisa crested the lip of the tunnel. She braced her elbows on the floor with the rest of her body dangling in the hole. Half her weight still rested on the smart rope though her foot.

The room was empty. The smoldering remains of a scout lay in the corner. Telisa remembered to look up. A tan shape darted above. She yanked the trigger of the smart pistol. The shot echoed in the tiny room. As soon as she did it, some part of her mind told her to use the link command next time to increase her accuracy.

There were scraps of wood and fabric obscuring parts of the ceiling, almost like hammocks, and the wide flower of a glue grenade covered one full quarter of the ceiling. There were lumps under it, but they looked just like more of the surviving Konuan structures. Telisa lowered her head slightly and raised the pistol, ready to fire again. A soft scraping noise echoed through the room.

Why can I always hear it and never see it?

"Cilreth, is that you?" she sent through her link.

The other scout robot emerged from the tunnel beside Telisa. She heard the high-pitched whine of a stunner as the scout shot toward the ceiling. Telisa heard a scratching noise again.

Did Cilreth go back? Why isn't she answering me?

A long spear shape descended from the ceiling, then opened into an umbrella over the scout almost before it could register on Telisa's eyes. The speed was startling, scary.

Telisa released a shot at the creature as she told the ascender to free-fall. She didn't stay to see if the smart round struck the thing. It had a target profile specifying any non-human as a legal target, so it probably wouldn't fly through a grille and hit Cilreth, wherever she was.

If she's still alive.

"Cilreth?" Telisa transmitted.

Of course. Cilreth activated her stealth suit. She might still have been in the room! But she would have answered.

A noise behind her dispelled all thoughts of going back to find Cilreth.

That thing is coming, and it's fast. Is it a Konuan, or is it...what the grilles were supposed to keep out?

She thought about the spear shape that had opened, umbrella-like, over the scout. It looked like it could have fit through the grille, from her instant impression of it.

Telisa sprinted down the tunnel. She had no idea where she was going, but she slid the lightning gun off her back and grasped its two odd, vaselike handles. The heavy device took both her hands to aim and activate. Then she turned.

Let's see it deal with this!

She didn't see a target. Nevertheless, she almost pulled the trigger, figuring the guided missiles would find their own targets, likely to include the Konuan or Konuan predator. Then she thought of Cilreth again. The gun could easily kill both Cilreth and the alien creature, even if they were still back in the room. Telisa and Shiny hadn't yet figured out how to keep the alien weapon from harming friends.

Open the range.

"Come on!" she yelled out. "Come get me. I'm down here!"

Then she ran farther down the dark tunnel. Her light dangled at her belt. She turned it on with her link, but the rays scattered across the floor around her rather than illuminating what was directly ahead.

"Cilreth, I don't know if you can hear me, but if you can, run back the way we came. I'm going to kill the thing."

She activated a night vision suite, but an infrared view wasn't very useful either. The tunnel's temperature was too uniform. She turned to look back. A huge manta ray of a creature opened right next to her like a giant flower opening for the sun.

Three Entities—!

She felt air move by her head. Then the creature fell away. Telisa ran again. She held onto the weapon in one hand and grabbed her flashlight in the other.

It must have been a Vovokan sphere that saved me.

The tunnel was smooth, slightly blue, but Telisa was only paying attention to where it led. She saw another source of light ahead. She let the flashlight dangle again and grabbed the weapon in both hands. She looked back. A single Vovokan guardian sphere trailed her, but there was no sign of the other.

Telisa slowed as she neared the end of the tunnel. A wide room opened ahead. She took another step forward. The room beyond the tunnel looked circular. She saw two banks of equipment or large machines on the far side.

Trilisk. They looked just like the dead hulks they had seen on Thespera. But this time, she saw blinking lights on the surfaces ahead. Cool air moved across the skin of her face.

She stepped through the tunnel and into the room. Four smooth blue columns obscured the corners. The looked very similar to the columns they had found around the trap on Thespera. Trilisk machines.

The air felt different. Electric. Telisa reached for something in her pack, then decided against it.

I'm being hunted by a Konuan so I stop to analyze the air? Then I get eaten.

She checked behind her. No signs of pursuit. The tunnel she had entered by was utterly dark. She tried her flashlight, but it didn't travel far down the tunnel. She still didn't see anything. The light had a weak laser option, but she didn't want to attract anything.

Of course it knows which way I went. There weren't any other turns. Or were there?

She wondered if the Vovokan sphere was back there blocking it, or if the sphere was destroyed, the creature cowed…no way of knowing. They hadn't worked out the attendant-link integration far enough for Telisa to ask her current attendant what had happened to the other one.

Telisa accessed her Vovokan sphere. She had a few canned commands available to use. She told it to sweep the room. Telisa remained in place, holding the weapon. If the sphere flushed anything out, she would be ready. The sphere took off, slipping behind the column to her left. She watched the feed through her link. The column had a few more cables or tubes on the far side, a couple of dim lights, but nothing else. There wasn't a place for anything to hide.

The sphere continued. Telisa just stood by. She turned with her back to the pillar the sphere had checked, sideways to the tunnel. The Vovokan sphere revealed another smooth blue tunnel, also dark, leaving from behind the second pillar. Then another from behind the third pillar.

So the room is roughly square, but I'm at the intersection of three tunnels.

"I wish I still had two guardian spheres," she said aloud. She thought of prayer machines again, but she dismissed it. She had already tried that just above.

Ah, but the Trilisks might have wanted it for themselves and screened it from above, just as Shiny kept the AI he found from working in his enemies' houses.

"I want a knife," Telisa said. She knelt down and placed her pack on the ground. She imagined a solid, shiny metal blade and a soft rubber handle. "I really need a knife in my pack."

She glanced down the tunnel again, saw nothing, then opened her pack. She found only her supplies inside.

Dammit. I've been forever spoiled. I'm going to travel all over the galaxy and every now and then try a prayer and see if it works! I can see how humans got hooked on this stuff.

She replaced the alien weapon on her back. Then she clutched the breaker claw in one hand and her smart pistol in the other. Her imagination brought up an image of the Trilisk machine they had discovered…the trilateral symmetry and its dark sapphire coloration.

If those machines are running, then what if robots are, too?

Telisa froze and just listened for a moment.

What if I accidentally kill a Trilisk robot with the breaker and cause an interspecies incident? Or at least a species to robots-of-extinct-species incident…

Telisa pushed down the negative thoughts and simply examined the room as the Vovokan satellite lazily floated around her. The columns had no manual controls. Typical of Trilisk machines. The center of the room was raised in a circular shape, a kind of low dais only a small step above the rest of the floor. The floor was clean, too clean. Some kind of system had to be in operation to prevent the accumulation of dirt or dust.

Always they have these columns. And almost nothing else. No bedrooms, bathrooms, meeting chambers, nothing to really tell me more. The robot we found is an exception.

I wonder if the space force ever found one. I wonder if it's actually a dead Trilisk cyborg.

Telisa felt a stab of guilt. She had no idea if Cilreth was still alive, if the monster was still coming, but here she stood, wondering about the Trilisks. She decided she had to choose a tunnel and try to get back.

Telisa stepped onto the dais. Suddenly she felt light-headed.

"Wha—"

She lost her balance and collapsed.

Chapter 11

Holtzclaw walked through the haphazard clusters of alien buildings behind his men. The surface of his battle suit maintained the broken red color of the rocks and walls around him. He was in constant communications with his surveillance team, the Hellraker operator, and his mission group.

His battle suit was simply a powered exoskeleton mated to a military grade skinsuit and a helmet. It increased his mass by about 50 percent, but that was not a problem moving across the hard, rocky landscape. Originally the battalion had an exoskeleton only for each officer, squad leader, and the heavy weapon operator, but almost all the men had them now. One of the few advantages of heavy attrition of the unit: the exoskeletons had survived more often than the men had.

"Any activity back at their ship?" he asked. Though he could see the ship in one of the panes of his personal view, he relied upon his men to sift through details and notice things he would miss while his attention was divided.

"Quiet. Something's not right about it, though. This ship is nothing like I've ever seen."

"It must be some fancy science mission one-off," Holtzclaw said.

"Yes, sir. You got the fancy part right. It looks like it took some serious landing prep just to set it down. Some kind of surface construction to make a place to sit its fat ass down planet-side."

Holtzclaw looked at the ship again. His man was right. The ship was radical. He couldn't even see any ramps or means of ingress. The landing site had several pre-built spots to support the struts.

We must have missed some probe that arrived ahead of time to construct those landing pads. "Well, it's about to be our fancy ship," he said.

Holtzclaw trailed the center of his advancing mission group. He had mobilized eight squads of five men each. A Guardian machine had been assigned to each of the squads. Though the Guardians had been designed for perimeter security, they could be useful in a frontal assault.

The Hellrakers were set up and on high alert, but he preferred to capture everything intact. More supplies for him that way. If they encountered any resistance, he was ready to use up Hellraker rounds in exchange for whatever was on that big fat ship they had seen come down. There were probably literally years' worth of supplies and equipment on that vessel. And if it was a science expedition, it could be invaluable in trying to figure out what they hauled out of the tunnels.

The rest of his soldiers were taking off in the next few minutes to challenge any assets the strangers had left in orbit. As with the ground attack, their orders were to capture what they found rather than destroy it. Holtzclaw had put Silvarre in charge of their assault craft.

On the ground, his men were spread across a two-kilometer line north to south, moving to the east. Sensor probes moved in the same direction, two to the south and one to the north. Even though he expected all the action to take place topside today, he had a moment of pause thinking about the engineers he had left behind. They had sheltered underground to defend themselves against the monster. If it chose to strike now, it could be bad. But at least he had told them to remain vigilant. There were limited avenues of attack in the long tunnels.

"We have a robot here, headed away from us."

"Kill it," Holtzclaw said. "Neutralize all their machines. Take the scientists alive unless they resist with arms."

There was a pause.

"Got it. Target is down."

A minute later, squad three, farther to the south, got another one. And another. Holtzclaw discovered the machines were armed when the third one shot back. None of his men were injured, and they killed it easily.

They're not prepared for this. They're no match for us.

For another half hour they swept across the old city. They killed a fourth robot in the north; then Holtzclaw got a transmission. He caught a visual feed of the officer. A long, straight nose divided the heavily lined face above compressed lips. It was First Lieutenant Racca.

"We have a couple of robots holed up in a building," the officer said.

"Any people in there?"

"No, sir, not unless they've got stealth hardware. The probes are sure it's just robots. There's at least two of them sheltering in there," Racca said. "We could use a Guardian machine, but I thought, maybe this would be a good test for our Hellraker calibration?"

"Yes, good thinking," Holtzclaw agreed. The Guardian ammunition had also gotten pretty low, because those machines had been taking pot shots at the Konuan for weeks. His unit needed resupply or access to manufacturing resources they could use to produce more ammunition. Their assault ships had basic fabrication systems that could be used in a pinch, though they were slow and out of certain raw materials. The fabrication systems were meant to construct critical replacement parts for the ships in emergencies, not to supply a battalion with ammunition. Not even a heavily attritioned battalion like theirs.

Holtzclaw received a location pointer from Racca and passed it on. He announced the target on the mission channel. The fire system verified all friendlies were clear of the target.

"Incoming," said the Hellraker operator.

Michael McCloskey

Holtzclaw accessed a visual feed from one of the probes on the line. A small Konuan building sat in a clearing. Nothing moved, but his men were sure at least two of the machines were inside.

Three seconds later the dwelling blossomed into a gigantic cloud of red dust rising into the sky. The thunder came seconds later. Holtzclaw wasn't sure if he could feel the tremor or if it was imagined.

"Direct hit," Holtzclaw heard.

Good to know everything is still in working order. "Resume the advance," he said. The squads started advancing again.

Holtzclaw's link announced a communication channel opening from his task force newly arrived in orbit.

"Colonel Holtzclaw, this is the *Typhoon*."

"Report," he said.

"There's another very large ship here, just like the first one," Silvarre said. "We're closing in on it, but I have to tell it to you straight, sir, I doubt a ship of that size—"

Silvarre's voice feed cut out.

"Silvarre? Major?"

There was no answer.

I doubt a ship of that size...what?

"Major Silvarre?"

I doubt a ship of that size isn't armed.

Holtzclaw tried to get the *Typhoon*'s beacon. There was nothing. Which meant the ship had gone dark to avoid attack, or it had been destroyed. The other two ships, *Scion* and *Griffin*, were silent as well. His forces in space were engaged.

"Step it up," Holtzclaw sent to his squad leaders. "We have trouble in orbit. I want that ship."

Chapter 12

Magnus had turned the stealth machine off long before he approached the campsite where he had left Telisa and Cilreth. His nighttime journey had been hard on the nerves, but otherwise uneventful. If anything, the planet life seemed less active at night. It was possible the majority of species here were diurnal.

The first thing that worried him was a lack of scout machines around the camp. He moved through the last patches of native plant life carefully but didn't encounter any sentries.

The tent was sealed up. To be expected for the middle of the night.

"Telisa? Cilreth?" he transmitted. For a second there was no reply.

"Magnus! I'm glad you're back," Cilreth said. Magnus could tell something was wrong. Her voice held a worry. He strode up to the tent as she gave the mental signal for the tent to open.

"Magnus, we were attacked," she said aloud. "I've been trying to reach you and Shiny for half an hour."

Distressed but not panicked.

"Tell me."

"We took some scout robots to the ruins. We found this robot." Cilreth indicated a smooth blue machine with three legs sitting beside a stack of containers. "Some creature attacked us. It destroyed two scouts. Telisa and I were separated as we fought. It's my fault, a glitch with the suit. I had to activate the stealth, but then it wasn't configured to give me away by showing my link, and I was having a hard time staying alive and configuring it to let me talk to her. She told me to clear away, said she was going to kill it."

Magnus nodded. "Okay. Maybe she meant her alien weapon. She was worried about hitting you. Did you hear it fire?"

"No. But she was on the level below me." Cilreth sent him a location pointer as she spoke so he wouldn't have to ask the obvious. The spot wasn't far from the camp.

Oh no. And I have her stealth device. Magnus felt ashamed. She needed that artifact and he'd taken it from her. Now she could be dead.

"Magnus, it's fast. And it attacks from above."

"Okay, stay calm, I'll go get her; you get what we can back onto the ship. Prioritize the loading; we may be leaving some of this stuff behind. You should find a large group of scout machines waiting back at the *Clacker* that got cut off from us. Use them to move as much as you can, as fast as you can."

"Magnus? Are you okay?"

"I've figured out why we can't talk with Shiny. It's bad."

"It can't be worse than abandoning my teammate to an alien monster."

"It's not your fault. Don't even start that or I'll hit you. We just need to find her."

"Then go!"

"Yes. One minute. The people here are UED. Looks like a military unit, too. More than a hundred of them, I'd guess. They're situated less than ten kilometers away."

"So close! Did they follow us in?"

"Their camp suggests they were here first. They had to have detected us come in. My guess is they're jamming our links. Our current range is less than about forty meters."

"What can we do about them? Are they dangerous?"

"Maybe. I haven't contacted them. Keep an eye out. They may be after the *Clacker*." Magnus found more weapon containers with his link. He spoke as he grabbed some grenades and a laser sidearm.

"Maybe we should talk to them," Cilreth said.

"What are you thinking? The enemy of my enemy?" Magnus asked.

"Sure."

Magnus shrugged. "They aren't really our friends. They have their own agenda. Besides, we're fugitives from the space force, but we're not really revolutionaries, are we?"

"I might change things if I felt I could," Cilreth said. "I think Telisa would. Though I don't want to rock the boat just now, if the aliens really are a huge threat."

Magnus hurried off but continued talking through his link, knowing the jamming would cut their connection soon. Three scout robots near the camp scampered after him. "Earth and the other core worlds are all stirred up about it, but I think it was just a chance encounter that went bad. But the Earth Defiance has lost. The space force all but mopped them up years ago."

"Propaganda? Maybe the war is still going on."

"Well, not from where I was sitting," Magnus pointed out. "But I suppose there could have been more of them out on the frontier than the force let me know about."

"Shiny knows what it's like when an alien race comes for your home planet. We can't let that happen to Earth. Or any core world. If the UED is still in action, we can't join them now."

The aliens will always be out there. I hope that doesn't mean we have to live with an oppressive government forever. "We can talk about it when we join back up with Telisa."

"Possible workarounds, countermeasures, antidotes to apply. Implementing solutions now," Shiny's voice interrupted on a new channel. His voice was of obviously lower quality in the transmission.

Magnus halted just within range of Cilreth.

"Shiny. Take over the scout robots if you can contact them. Coordinate a defense with them. Telisa is missing. I'm going to find her," he rattled off.

"Cannot contact Telisa. Caution advised. There is…" Shiny broke up. "…Trilisk technology involved."

"Repeat," Magnus asked, but he lost the connection. *Classic. A warning so fragmented it is unusable other than to inspire fear.*

"It's a good sign he could reach us at all," Cilreth said. "If anyone can defeat the jamming, it has to be Shiny. Just find Telisa."

"I should not have separated from her," Magnus said, resuming his departure. He encountered a communications repeater service up ahead. "This repeater is ours?" he asked.

"Oh yes, sorry, I forgot about the breadcrumbs. We have them out all the way to the building. She's still alive," Cilreth continued. "She has a lot of alien toys, remember? She's just too naive. Shiny could be dangerous, too. Telisa is too young to have felt enough sting from betrayal or double-crossing to think of it seriously."

Magnus accessed the breadcrumb's service and joined the chain. "Yes. But her youth brings a lot to the team. I like being around her." *Of course, I love her. Why do I hesitate to say that in front of Cilreth?*

"You like that young bod," Cilreth prodded.

"It's more than that. She keeps us enthusiastic, injects optimism and energy. Being around young people reminds you of the hopeful side of things."

"Then maybe we need some more. Just three of us…"

"Yes. I'm working on that. But it's on the back burner. After this expedition, we should at least double the size of our team. That would give each of us a new protégé to teach. If you're not in this area, we'll head back to the ship.

Most likely Shiny will have defeated the jamming before then, anyway."

"Okay. Be careful, Magnus. Bring her back."

Magnus increased his pace. He didn't want to be winded when he arrived, but he could make good time without undue fatigue. The lack of sleep might become more of an issue. He had his suit dispense a stimulant into his bloodstream. Then he followed a map toward the location Cilreth had provided. The breadcrumb devices verified his route.

Very useful little things during a communications blackout.

He found a hole in the wall of a building close to the spot. The chips of the wall next to a removed grille were a slightly different color of red than the surface of the wall or the rocks below, so they had probably been made recently.

They came in this way.

Magnus turned on a light, clipped it to his rifle, and dove through the hole.

I need to find Telisa...alive.

Michael McCloskey

Chapter 13

Arakaki moved slowly across the ruins after the Konuan.

She didn't have any delusions about who hunted whom. The Konuan was letting her follow. It wanted to lure her out away from her friends, her Guardians, and her probes. It planned to ambush and kill her just as it had done to so many of her fellow soldiers.

I'm coming, you bastard.

Arakaki checked her PAW for the tenth time. Its self-diagnostic reported optimal. The laser at her hip verified at full charge over her link. All her grenades checked in, including the one around her throat. The UED probe taking up the rear thirty meters behind her monitored the area. It reported another sensor ghost near a larger building ahead.

So this is the spot for your trap. Fine.

It had steadily led her across half the city, going toward the area occupied by the newcomers and their tiny robots. Arakaki figured the Konuan must be hunting them as well. At least she hoped it was. Anything to distract its predation of the UED unit would be a welcome break.

Or so I tell myself. Have I grown so used to it being out there, hunting, that I would miss it? Miss my chances to kill it or die trying?

She chomped down painfully on the sliver in her mouth. The tiny fragment was so tough she could gnaw on it for decades without accomplishing anything but wearing her teeth.

Arakaki dropped the self-analysis and walked toward the building.

"Captain Arakaki, report," Holtzclaw ordered over the link.

"I'm pursuing the Konuan," she said. She half expected to be chewed out for calling for fire support, or to be pulled away for another remote pickup. But Holtzclaw had something completely different cooking.

"Good. Keep on it. Keep that thing away from camp. I've pulled a lot of men and probes to go after the science ship east of the ruins. Our tech team is vulnerable in the back."

"Yes, sir."

That suited Arakaki. She was seldom so happy to have to obey. Especially since she had given up all hope for the war. She had contemplated desertion several times, but…where would she go? What would she do without him? And here, she had the creature to hunt.

In another five minutes she saw the first face of the structure. Like all the other clusters of Konuan living chambers, it was a hodgepodge of square cells heaped one upon another three or four layers above ground. There was often one layer under the surface as well, and below that, Trilisk tunnels.

There was a hole in the side of the building. Arakaki looked at the roof and clusters of plants nearby. She didn't sense any danger. Neither did the probe trailing her. She padded over to the opening.

Arakaki checked the rocky ground. There was no dirt to hold any prints, but the red coating on the rocks became darker if their surface was recently scuffed or struck. The rocks around the entrance held a lot of evidence of movement through the area. She spotted some wide scuffmarks—Terrans'—as well as the smaller pick holes caused by the spider legs of their little robots.

Who are these people? Scouts? Scientists? Why are there so few of them? They said the ship was huge.

The UED soldier knelt beside the entry point. She listened and scanned. Her weapon picked up a power signature. A machine. It could be a piece of equipment or a robot. It wasn't moving though.

They left something behind here. Maybe some poor sucker was carrying something, the Konuan got him, and he dropped whatever he was carrying.

Her curiosity had been awakened. A Konuan trap? Unlikely. It had never used such tactics before, at least not that anyone had survived to report. The creature was always certain to destroy the link in its victim. It was scary to think it knew that would limit their knowledge of it.

Arakaki dropped to the ground. Her dark gray battle suit protected her from the cold, hard stone. She crawled forward, weapon first, toward the hole left by the pulled grille. The probe covered her back. She hoped it would be enough warning if the Konuan darted in from behind to attack her.

She saw it. A silvery metal ant the size of a large dog. It stood near the center of a room filled with rusted strips of metal hanging from walls and ceiling.

The machine turned toward her. There was a split second where she had the choice to fire first. She decided against it. Some part of her knew instantly that her target was the Konuan, not these odd robots.

The machine didn't fire at her.

As I thought. It's got weapons, but not for me.

Then she scolded herself slightly. If the machine had shot a glue grenade at her, she could have been pinned here like food on a dinner plate awaiting the Konuan's pleasure.

But of course I have the ace up my sleeve...or around my neck.

"So, you're not going to shoot me?" she said quietly. She left her weapon aimed at the machine and slid forward through the low portal. The floor inside was a bit below ground level. She regained her footing.

The machine turned back toward one of the other openings and froze. Arakaki gave the room a once-over. She didn't see anything Terran looking except the robot. It was definitely responsible for the power signature: the machine had a lot of juice. At its current output, Arakaki doubted it could go for more than a few hours.

Arakaki's own weapon angled toward the same doorway the machine covered.

Do we have company?

Her weapon didn't see any other targets. The probe trailing Arakaki sidled up outside the building. It was a tall cylinder about a quarter of a meter in diameter adorned with countless ports, sensors, and sampling equipment. The machine gently hovered outside, then settled onto the red rocks to save energy. It wouldn't go through the doorway by itself, even though it could theoretically fit through if turned on its side. The machine could only hover in an upright position, so Arakaki would have to lug it through herself if she wanted it inside the building. Even if she were willing to make that investment, it would have to be repeated for every new room. She left the probe outside. It could still pick up a lot through the walls of the Konuan ruin, since it had extremely sensitive sonic sensors and radiation scanners.

Whoever owns the bug here knows I've arrived. Unless the Konuan already got them.

Only one of the grilles in the room had been opened. So if one of the scientists had been here, they went that way, or they went to a lot of trouble to make it look that way.

Just to be sure, Arakaki checked the other grilles. With her weapon ready, she pulled on them one at a time and examined them for signs of tampering. The other exits looked solid, and she didn't find any signs of the Konuan. The probe outside told her the adjacent rooms were clear.

Which proves almost nothing, she thought to herself. She prepared to slide through the grille hole into the next room straight ahead.

Arakaki stole a glance back at the bug. The machine didn't move.

"Guarding the door, huh? Good luck with that," Arakaki murmured. She turned back to the room. She saw silvery webs of metal gleaming on the walls.

What the hell?

Arakaki grabbed a grenade as she stared for a couple seconds, trying to figure out what the structures were. She saw the flash of a furry, umbrella-shaped body flitting away like a squid swimming through the air. At the same moment the probe notified her link of a reading. She didn't hesitate. She tossed her incendiary grenade to the ground and gave it a destination in the adjacent chamber to her left.

It's too fast. I'll aim where it isn't.

The grenade whirred through the grille and into the side room. There, it took the next right and rolled through another grille.

Blam! Blam!

Arakaki sent a couple of rounds from her PAW straight ahead to run the creature toward her seeker grenade coming in from the side. The thing might well go in another direction, but she had to try.

A massive flower of flame erupted from the grille opening. A redundant detonation report from the grenade arrived at her link. She stepped aside a bit late. Her face burned. Then just as quickly as the heat had come, it dissipated.

The summary result was *target grazed.* The grenade's computer brain, at least, believed in its last instant of existence it would slightly damage the enemy. Arakaki had set all her weapons slightly on the "trigger happy" side, knowing the Konuan was a fast and resourceful target.

Her probe lost track of the creature again. But Arakaki felt sure it wasn't dead.

No, I didn't get it. This is just the beginning.

Michael McCloskey

Chapter 14

Telisa's consciousness resumed.

Something is very, very wrong.

Her link did not respond. Her surroundings were dim. Small spots of light floated randomly about the room. Her eyesight failed her in the darkness, but she could smell the rock walls and she could hear air moving through the grilles nearby. These clues brought her to the conclusion: she was inside one of the cube-shaped Konuan rooms.

She tried to move her head. It didn't go well. Her head had melted into a flat mass. She took a deep breath. She had no lungs. She only heard a loud rustling.

What is that? WHAT HAS HAPPENED?

Telisa tried to stand. She moved forward. She could tell it was moving forward, but she didn't have two long, strong legs. She had a dozen. A hundred. More.

Oh, by the Five! I'm one of the banana slugs. This is just a bad dream. It has to be. The technology required—Trilisk. Nonono…

Telisa paused to calm down. She tried to breathe again. Instead of the familiar feel of air bags expanding in her chest, tiny flaps of flesh—gills?—vibrated beneath her, causing the rustling sound again.

Can this body even handle distress? I could have the slug equivalent of a heart attack and die. No. Most organisms must be able to handle a bit of fear. Unless I got a damaged or frail body. Just don't panic.

Telisa tested her legs. Yes, hundreds of them now. She experimented. She could move just one, if she tried. It was like wiggling a toe. She scratched the rock wall. Despite the tiny victory of control, despair railed through her.

What am I going to do? It's not a recording. I'm living this.

Telisa decided to try and look around. She could only see in four small, hand-sized spots that roved about the room. It was like four small flashlights moving about.

Wait. I am controlling those with my...arms. My arms are flashlights. Five Entities, hear me!

The words came to mind of their own accord. When Telisa was scared, really scared, she talked more like her mother, more like she had when she was a little girl. But she was old enough to know now that the only thing getting her out of this predicament was herself or her team. Unless, of course, a Trilisk prayer device was operating within range.

Change me back now. I want my old body back.

Nothing happened. But she remembered her friends. Maybe they could help. Magnus. Or Shiny or Cilreth. If they didn't shoot her on sight.

The room had some bits of cloth and rotten plant stalks on a wall. They had been glued in place, or...for some reason they just sat there. A few rods stuck out of the walls. Then Telisa realized she had misoriented herself.

The plant stalks were sitting on the floor. She wasn't.

I'm already on the wall. I'm clinging to the wall. I'm crawling on the Five Times Accursed wall.

Telisa just sat there and waited to adjust further.

Get it together. Just get it together, dammit.

Her sight was abysmal. The colors were washed out. Or maybe she just couldn't see red anymore. But her *hearing.* Telisa could hear everything around her in the sharpest detail. Her tiny claws scraping against the stone. A drip of moisture that must be fifty meters away. In fact, she could tell it was about fifty meters away just by the way it sounded.

She crawled forward a little more. Her legs coordinated themselves. It made her feel more in control to move. Somehow, she didn't have to think about how to coordinate the legs. It felt natural. She focused on the far wall. She could feel coiled power in her body.

Telisa sprang off the wall. Several things happened at once. When she launched, her body folded quickly like an umbrella, forming a torpedo shape that cut effortlessly through the air. She felt muscles or their equivalent compressing the trapped air, squeezing it out of her collapsing body to help accelerate. One of her arms seemed to point ahead to light the way for her eyes all by itself. Then she was flying through the air, effortlessly, like a missile in slow motion. She seemed to fly for a long time, though it could only have been a fraction of a second. Like a tumbler, her body swung around as she traveled, timed perfectly to land on her legs at the destination.

Just before landing, she popped back open with a snap, decelerating as the air cushion trapped between her opening body and the wall pressurized. Her wiry legs absorbed the last of the impact, what little there was left at the moment of landing. And there she was, one second later, on the opposite wall.

Banana slug, my ass. Let's see a slug hop across the room like that!

Telisa felt like a combination grasshopper-bat. Instead of two giant hopping legs, she had dozens. *Instinctual movement? But I'm Terran. My brain is Terran. It was Terran. How do I know how to jump like a Konuan? The Trilisk machine just...endowed me with these abilities? How could such a thing be translated? How can I still be thinking like myself at all? Same software, different hardware? Impossible.*

Telisa hopped back to the other side of the room.

Not impossible. Very, very difficult. Very, very amazing. And the Trilisks knew how to do it.

The exhilaration of jumping made her feel just a bit better. And more in mastery of her own fate. Telisa couldn't see anything interesting in the room. No clues as to how she had arrived. She crawled toward the nearest grille. She arrived atop the grill, then realized she couldn't fit through the vertical vents from the top. She had to approach from the side, where the long openings would accept her wide body. Then she just slipped through. It was effortless.

Okay, well, the grilles are indeed just doorways. And having more than one slit means that more than one Konuan can enter or leave at the same time. Any non-Konuan probably can't follow, though; neither can bulky objects be moved about.

The next room had tiny square pits in the floor filled with ash. Horizontal metal rods were affixed a couple of centimeters from the walls. The ceiling had vents. Telisa assumed it was some kind of cooking or smoking chamber. She moved for another grille, trying to find her way outside by listening to the air movements around her.

Something abruptly changed. Telisa stopped, overwhelmed by a new sensation. She felt a flood of new impulses coming from…the surface under her feet. She brought her tiny lights to bear but saw nothing.

I can sense…a trail…smell? Touch?

The sensation had a direction. Forward and to the right. She followed the trail into the next room. It was a mostly empty cube filled with garbage. Dust that might have once been wood or cloth or paper sat in piles with bits of rusted metal. The trail led onward.

It could be a trap. Maybe the other Konuan is luring me.

Telisa slowed but did not stop. What alternative did she have? She tried to rustle her breathing flaps more quietly and listened to the world. If she couldn't see well, she would have to rely more upon her hearing to sense danger.

On a whim she walked in a circle, then checked her own trail. It was just as strong, but smelled subtly different.

So. I leave the same scent trail. The other Konuan can follow me easily, too.

Telisa followed the trail through two more rooms, when it abruptly ended. She looked around with her washed-out vision. She didn't see anything except another cubical room.

Oh, of course. It leaped from here. To…where?

Finally her poor vision noticed a circular well in the floor instead of a grille.

An entrance to the Trilisk tunnels.

Telisa crawled all about until she found a spot where the Konuan before her had landed. It *had* been a jump that broke the trail. She followed the line. It had jumped here, and then…? Probably into the tunnel below. Telisa crawled down to check. She put half her body down the well and walked around the rim. She could smell it. This is where it had gone, into the Trilisk tunnels.

With a shrug that could only be imagined, Telisa crawled over the edge of the well and downward. Despite the smooth surface of the well, her legs stuck to the sides. She moved over the metal without fear of falling.

The tunnel below smelled very different to her Konuan feet. Clean and metallic.

Of course. I smell through my feet. Sigh.

Her gill flaps rustled.

I try to sigh, and it causes this new body to breathe. I try to move forward and my hundreds of legs just do it. It has all been connected in a way to minimize the alien-ness of the transfer. Yet a change this radical remains profound. One can't be perfectly mapped from Terran to Konuan. It all just feels right. Masterful.

The bottom of the well smoothly joined into a horizontal tunnel. Telisa followed the trail onto the ceiling of the tunnel and crawled on. She slowed. A new sensation had started to build. Some of her legs were not working. She felt them clutching onto something instead. Many somethings. She held many tiny orbs to her body with at least a dozen legs.

What are those? Eggs? I don't understand. This is less than masterful.

Telisa tried to release one. She couldn't quite force herself to let it go. She didn't want to let them go. Somehow the deposits had become so very *important.*

Unbelievable. I don't understand my own physiology enough to even get by. It could be dangerous. This could be a symptom of not breathing right, not eating, drinking, even standing upside down too long.

Telisa could not bring herself to drop anything so she simply walked on. A few more of her legs became distracted by the tiny spheres.

They have to be coming from me. This ceiling is utterly clean.

She came to a three-way intersection of the tunnels. Staying on the ceiling, she entered a triangular shaped space that joined the tunnels. There was a niche in the three corners of the ceiling. Telisa was drawn to one of the tiny protected spaces. She flowed over it, covering the depression with her body.

She shook. Her legs spasmed. Telisa couldn't think about anything; she just *was* for a moment. Then she focused on the smell of the spheres. Several of her legs ticked out to tap the walls of the niche. Then she put one of the orbs there. Somehow, it stuck to the wall.

Then she placed another, and another.

Well, at least I know what to do with them now. Less to carry...Five Entities.

Her legs started to work rapidly. More and more of the tiny modules became affixed to the surfaces of the niche as she worked. Time became meaningless. Finally she seemed to come back into focus.

I can move away now.

She flowed forward from the niche, then turned about to take a look. Her eyesight was poor, but it looked like she had deposited at least a hundred little black nodules, maybe more.

If this is what my life has become, I'm not going to be sane much longer.

She attempted to dispel the negative thoughts.

I'm going to get help. Shiny could help. Or I can figure out that Trilisk platform and get back to my regular self.

Telisa found the trail again and continued. She had to be following a chemical trail like an ant following a predecessor. The trails would help her to find another Konuan. But now she wondered: Did she really want to find the one that hunted them? Wouldn't it be deadly? Or did it only kill Terrans?

If I can follow it, then it can follow me. If it finds those egg-things, it might fertilize them. Or maybe they are clones of me. Or maybe they are just chunks of excrement. This is miserable.

Telisa left the intersection on the trail and left by another corridor. It was long and straight like the last one. The trail started out in parallel with the tunnel on the ceiling, but after some distance, which was hard for Telisa to estimate, it veered left.

Telisa noticed something. A tiny crack. She would have missed it as a Terran. To a Konuan, it was like a canyon. As soon as she started to crawl across it, she could feel it there.

Why did the tunnel have a seam? An artifact of modular construction?

No. Trilisk stuff is made perfectly, designed down to the molecular level. No such thing as an accidental or incidental seam in their work. It's a doorway.

She searched the large square panel that curved with the surface of the cylindrical tunnel. There were no buttons or levers. Only the perfect seam around the entire perimeter.

Open?

The panel started to slide open. Telisa hopped off it instantly in a startled reaction.

Wow. I'm fast.

She felt elation that the panel had opened to her mere mental command. Either that, or something else had opened it...Telisa listened. The sound of the mechanism sliding the door was like thunder to her fine hearing. She looked through the doorway. She saw a small passageway leading into a hidden room. Telisa hopped through and landed on the wall as naturally as a Terran would have strode through on the smooth black floor.

The room beyond looked like a space force armory. A dozen rifles leaned against the wall. Bins of grenades. Five battle suits. Pieces of military robots. Explosives.

This is an incredible pile of tech. If this was gathered by the Konuan, it's no primitive.

Backdropped against it all, a large column extended from floor to ceiling. It looked out of place in the cubical room with grilles on each wall.

Trilisk. Jackpot!

Telisa scurried right up to it, then onto its surface almost without thinking. She felt the smooth surface with her surface-clinging legs. Her claw legs tapped it gently, feeling everything under the two square meters of her body surface.

This is creepy how fast I'm getting used to crawling all over everything.

Telisa crawled around it full circle in the space of a second.

I want to be myself again, Telisa thought. Nothing happened. Is anything there? *I want to switch back.*

Her desires were ignored. But she felt another crack in the surface under her feet.

Open.

The casing of the column started to drop. Telisa hopped aside effortlessly and watched from a nearby wall. Her dim vision showed her the column opened to reveal a workspace within. She immediately found a small screwdriver-shaped tool sitting on a flat surface in one of her arm lights. She hopped into the column and took a closer look.

The craftsmanship was perfect. It was shiny. It looked to be made of plastic and metal. It was very flat. Tiny loops of metal decorated its sides.

Wait a moment. It's so very flat. And those loops...

Telisa walked over it. She slid six legs through the loops and pulled it flush with her belly.

Fits like a glove! This is a Konuan tool. But it's so much more advanced than a sword or a simple mechanical device. It could even be beyond Terran technology.

She carefully moved the wand to one corner of her body so both ends pointed off away from her. Then half a dozen of her legs moved over its surface.

It has no manual controls. It must use a link of some kind. But I have no link.

Telisa felt immense frustration. *Why would I be put into this body without my link? Wouldn't inter-body travelers need their cybernetic enhancements to come with them?* Yet here she was, helpless in so many ways. Trapped in body she couldn't understand yet had some almost instinctual ability to operate, but without any means of interfacing electronically with anything advanced. She crawled about the space again, looking for more tools or hints as to what the owner did inside the column.

I want a link. I need to be able to interface with these things, she thought. Nothing happened. If a prayer device was active, it had been set to ignore her pleas.

The other Konuan has a link or something like it. It makes no sense. Has that creature actually advanced itself from early industrial age to this all by itself? Or was it a servant or slave of the Trilisks? How is it still alive? What does it want? And if it finds me here, is it going to kill me?

Chapter 15

Cilreth had the last load of cases loaded onto the four scout robots she had gathered. The tiny convoy headed back to the ship at her command as Chigran's star lightened the eastern horizon.

"Magnus? Telisa? Shiny?" she transmitted. No answer. "What the hell am I gonna do if no one shows up? Take off in the *Clacker* by myself?"

She sighed. Then the opposite thought struck her: What would she do if a lot of people showed up? Magnus had said the UED might be coming for the Clacker. There had been yesterday's huge cloud in the distance and the sound of thunder like a bomb. Should she lock herself inside? The Vovokan vessel was so advanced; maybe they would not be able to get in.

Right about now she wished she had grabbed those pills at the criminal's compound. With a thousand or so of those, she might be able to forget about everything for a while.

Cilreth wondered how long she had before the UED showed up. But she did not want to leave. She wanted to get her friends out of trouble. How could she help Magnus and Telisa?

Well, the bad guys already know we're here, she thought. Telisa had gone down into one of the Trilisk tunnels. They hadn't taken time to map them yet. Yet. The *Clacker* could probably perform the scan...or she might be able to accomplish it right here. She asked the cases for inventory. One of them had a seismic analyzer.

Cilreth dug out the analyzer and pulled it from its case. It was a tall, hourglass-shaped metal cylinder with a flat black top and bottom. The curved parts in the middle were silver. Her link found its activation service. She turned it on with a thought and placed it on the ground. It didn't sit very well on the ragged rocks. She went to the nearest plant and shined a light down into its fissure. There among the roots she saw soft black soil. A few scuttling creatures ran from her light.

"Wonderful," she said to herself. She dropped to the ground and put the device into the fissure. She had to put her entire arm deep into the hole to place it. She closed her eyes and pushed it into the soft dirt. Then it was over. She snatched her arm back up and rolled away from the rocky opening.

I hope no one is listening.

The machine sent out impulses into the ground from the plant well. The resulting scan was fuzzy but good enough to take a peek. Tunnels crisscrossed the area about eight meters under the surface. Cilreth focused on the building where she and Telisa had gotten separated.

The tunnel below branched in three directions. Cilreth decided she had no way to know which way Telisa went, not with the jamming going on. But assuming Telisa had the presence of mind to run towards the *Clacker*, she might have taken the tunnel leading…almost below her current camp. Cilreth followed the tunnel further. The next intersection was a building not far from the camp.

And it's toward the Clacker.

Cilreth ordered the scout robots to resume carrying the load back toward the ship. She walked alongside them, carrying two cases herself. Then she set the cases down to check her weapons. She thought of the thing again: fast, deadly.

"I'm no match for that thing. Next mission we need fighting machines," she vowed. But she knew she still had her stealth suit. And it had worked to get her away alive once.

"What now?" she asked herself aloud.

Hmm. Maybe Telisa didn't go far. I could look for her down there. Or her blood. Oh, by the Entities, I don't want to find her body.

Cilreth fidgeted with her stunner. Then she drew her machete.

"I'll never hit the bastard with this," she said. What other weapons did they have? Pistols, stunners, lasers, grenades, and swords. The thing was fast, so light, handheld weapons were the only thing she might hit with...unless....

Cilreth looked at the Trilisk corridors. Long and straight. Sometimes as long as half a kilometer.

Cilreth found another case. She took out a sniper's weapon: a powerful three-shot laser with a tripod and a scope. The weapon wasn't a rifle since it had no need for a long barrel, but it could deliver a lot of energy accurately at great distances.

Maybe I could kill it from a long ways away.

Cilreth tossed her machete to shed some weight and slid the three-shot over her shoulder. She left the case on the ground and gave the scout that had carried the rifle case one of her own containers. She told the scouts to carry the last load to the *Clacker*, then headed off toward the other building. She recalled her favorite danger mantra.

The twitch is already killing me anyway.

She left the tiny train of scouts and headed for the building. When she got there, she realized her oversight immediately. She faced an ancient wall with two of the grilles built into it. And she hadn't brought anything to dig them out with.

"You are the most miserable planner that ever existed," Cilreth said to herself. Telisa had been carrying Shiny's digging device at the time they separated. Cilreth considered her rifle. It was a high-powered weapon, but shooting each grille out would eat through her ammo quickly. The weapon was at least much quieter than Magnus's incredibly loud rifle.

"Okay, just check the perimeter first," she said, still angry at herself for forgetting about the grilles. She turned and looked all around for a moment. Without any scout machines nearby, it rested upon her to be more alert than ever.

Movement caught her eye. Another of the tree clumps was dropping green worms. In all the action, she had forgotten completely about the tiny things. She saw a small clear creature pluck up a worm and pull it back toward the fissure where the stalks emerged. Then she saw another do the same.

"Ah, when the worms move, it's feasting time—"

A huge creature registered on Cilreth's mind. It had been standing there the whole time, next to the shedding plant, though its coloration made it look like a stand of plants itself. It was a horror of knobby legs and green tufts, a lobster-like monster. Cilreth saw a terrifyingly wide trap of a mouth with a hundred tendrils along the top and bottom edges. She knew instantly, utterly, her life was in danger.

She raised her rifle, but the thing attacked first. Four long spikes shot out toward her as fast as arrows. She felt an impact on the front of her suit and another on the top of her right leg. She shot the laser but missed as something yanked her forward. The weapon had no seeking projectiles, and it was not configured to lock onto something that looked like a stand of plants.

Cilreth realized the spines it had shot toward her *were still attached* to the monster. A wail rose from her throat as the tendrils began to take up more slack.

The damn thing is reeling me in; then I go into that Venus flytrap mouth—

Terror turned into a cold need that set aside her emotions. The laser lined up for another shot. A powerful yank of the tendrils sent her hopping forward a meter. The thing was closer now, easier to hit…

She activated the fire command. This time she hit her mark. A third of the pack's charge went into cooking the creature from the inside out. It burst into flame and made a squeal grotesquely similar to that of a real lobster dropped into boiling water.

The tendrils' pull subsided as the thing died. Cilreth dropped onto her backside.

Shouldn't I feel pain? Have I been poisoned? Paralyzed?

Cilreth drew a deep breath. She heard a sound like a frightened schoolgirl. She looked down at herself. Two of the spikes were embedded in her, one in her chest and one in her leg. She looked away and closed her eyes. She couldn't feel the pain. It must be blocked out like the initial stage of a gunshot wound.

Oh no.

One shuddering breath later she looked again. She grabbed a spine and moved it a bit. The spines had hook tips, but they were caught in her suit, not her flesh. The last layer had protected her from the attack, but the biological spear hooks were caught on her suit.

She grabbed the one sticking from her chest and pulled. It was stuck firmly.

I didn't bring the damn machete. Holy Entities…

She did not lament long about the lack of a machete. She was still alive, and that was what was important. Cilreth came to her senses and considered her other equipment. There should be a smaller knife in her pack. She looked around for other creatures, but didn't see anything threatening. She flicked a green worm away in disgust.

Her pack slid off her back as she lay there, allowing her to search for the knife. She found the tool, then cut away the tendrils. They were strong but no match for the sharp alloy.

I should have gone back to the Clacker. *I should never have left it.*

The scare had been severe, but she had been lucky. She tried to calm her nerves. Telisa might still be depending on her. Once Cilreth cut herself free, she tried to work the spines out of her protection. As she worked she ran the suit diagnostic. It reported some damage but judged itself to remain 95 percent effective.

Once she dropped the spines free on the ground before her, thoughts of returning to the ship assailed her again. But she decided to keep looking for Telisa.

How much worse could it get? I don't want to find out.

She walked toward the next corner with her stunner in her hand. Her gaze even flitted upward occasionally, looking for anything lurking on the roof. The other wall of the building had one grille opening, but the grille was missing.

"Yes! Wait. Who did that?"

Cilreth checked over her shoulder, then took out a flashlight. She directed the powerful beam into the entrance. She saw just another ruined Konuan room. Scraps of cloth or paper, a few old plant stalks, and a small rock carved into something. Something with three arms and three legs.

Creepy.

Cilreth knelt down and slid through the entrance. She paused to let her eyes adjust. She examined the little statuette again.

Wait. That's important. It shows they knew the Trilisks were here. Either that, or it's a bizarre coincidence. If a child has twenty toy monsters, what are the chances one of them accidentally looks like the alien race living below her? Focus, Cilreth. Telisa needs you.

She checked her tunnel map in her link. Straight ahead. The grille that direction was missing, too.

Someone else has done this. But it looks like it was a long time ago.

She crawled through to the next room, and the next. All she saw was rotten garbage and a few old pieces of oxidized metal. She kept an eye out for more little statues, but she did not catch sight of anything similar. She came to the room above the tunnel.

The center of the room held a circular opening leading straight down. Just like where she had been separated from Telisa. As soon as she saw it, Cilreth nervously checked the ceiling. She started to shake.

Dammit, dammit, dammit. I'm such a damn coward.

She turned her stealth suit on to calm down. It helped a bit. The suit still had a lot of juice. She decided to leave it on as a crutch, at least until it showed a third of its energy store was expended. She would use it now to get a grip, but she would make sure and leave plenty for if, or when, she really needed it.

I'm not really an explorer. I'm just a private investigator. Of the deskbound type.

Cilreth had a smart rope in her pack. She took it out with her suit's ghostly outline service turned on in her PV, to help orient herself while invisible. The rope anchored itself and prepared to bring her down to the tunnel below.

She took a deep breath and descended.

At the bottom, Cilreth pulled the sniper rifle off her shoulder. She activated the scope with her link and flipped through various low-light options. She saw the tunnel ahead in various frequencies of light, but none of them revealed any potential dangers.

She followed the long, smooth tunnel. She kept flipping through low-light settings until she saw a light ahead. It came from a larger room at the end. She slowed as she approached. No sounds disturbed the long tunnel.

Cilreth raised the rifle before her and took one step at a time. The room looked smooth walled and of advanced make, as if constructed of one piece of metal or plastic. There was no dust. Everything there looked brand new.

The room had three pillars extending from floor to ceiling. Each column was black and silver, wide, way too thick for her to wrap her arms around. In fact, she felt threatened by the fact she couldn't see what might be hiding behind them. Two other tunnels exited the room.

Cilreth walked over to the nearest pillar. "Telisa, where the hell are you? I don't know anything about Trilisk stuff."

Cilreth examined the massive pillar. It was way overbuilt, simply thicker than a metal pillar would have to be to support the ceiling. The other three pillars were the same thickness. Cilreth carefully touched the surface. The metal was smooth but it didn't feel warm or cold.

"How can this be human body temperature? Ridiculous," she noted aloud. She tapped the surface. Did it sound hollow? She wasn't sure.

What's in there?

Cilreth felt a vibration. There was a sound. A low humming. She stepped away.

Suddenly the top of the pillar was dropping. Cilreth realized the surface had been moving from the moment she felt the vibration, but it had been so smooth she hadn't seen it moving. In the next second the top had dropped almost to the level of her head. Cilreth took several steps back and aimed her heavy laser.

What am I shooting at?

The pillar's outer clasp continued to drop. In another couple of seconds, she would know.

A clear tube had been revealed beyond the outer wall of the column. The last bit of the sheath sunk into the floor. It was filled with...

"Ugh," she grunted. "What *is* that crap? Green moss?"

The inside of the tube had been stuffed with a fluffy green material. The mass must have been more than her own weight, unless it was extremely light. The color was darker than the plants above, she decided. But the closer she looked, the more she realized the mass had shape.

A massive, three-legged, three-armed shape.

By the Five!

Cilreth's hands wavered wildly. She dropped the barrel of her compact rifle lower, then looked around the room in case she had been so taken aback that something had approached unnoticed. But it was only her, her two attendant spheres, the three covered pillars, and the massive, fuzzy green derelict in the tube.

If Telisa was running from that thing, she may have hidden in one of these. Shit. She may be suffocating in one right now. She could be in one of the other three!

She took a deep breath and tried to gather her wits yet again. Her shaking subsided. The thing in the tube, Trilisk or not, looked very dead. Rather crumpled toward the bottom of the tube and utterly still. Had the Trilisks looked like that in life?

Cilreth walked over to another of the massive cylinders.

"So, how did I do that?"

She touched the pillar. Then she spoke quietly, "What's inside?"

The hum returned. The pillar was opening.

This is madness. How can the Trilisks know how to interpret the brain of a Terran and open on command? It's not like vastly different creatures across the galaxy could possibly have any universal wiring or patterns that would allow a machine to simply—

This time the clear cylinder revealed was empty. It lit up with a violet outline of a human brain. The walls of the tube rotated with thousands of glowing symbols. Even as Cilreth watched, the brain pulsed with activity. She watched flashes of light dart here and there through the brain as the symbols danced across the surface of the tube.

A brain. My brain? It is showing me...it has analyzed me, read me; it understands me as easily as I can read a network service driver...

Cilreth realized she was standing, mouth open, weapon dangling from her hand like a mesmerized idiot.

"Telisa. Where's Telisa?" she asked the pillar.

The display shifted. A new shape appeared. It was a flat, complex creature. The rendering of the creature was transparent to display some of its inner workings. An apparent nervous system flashed green. Cilreth couldn't see any centralized brain; its nerves were laid out in a grid like some kind of well-organized electronics project.

"What? Telisa. Where is Telisa?"

The display didn't change. Cilreth looked at the creature. It was disgusting. A living carpet with a hundred crab legs. It had four foldable antennae on top and two long, sharp-ended drinking tubes tucked underneath its body like huge fangs.

That is nasty! It must be one of our Konuan.

"Show me Cilreth," she said as a test. The Terran brain display returned. There was no discernable change in the display. The brain continued to hum with activity. A few diagrams flashed by too quickly for her to understand.

Cilreth tried to reach Magnus. She couldn't get through. She prepared a message and told her link to send it as soon as any connection opened to Shiny or Magnus.

"I've found a series of complex metal tube machines. They are large enough to be used as a hiding spot. Telisa could be inside one. We should deploy some scouts to search for more of them," she recorded. Then she attached a target signature and coordinates of the device before her.

Shiny can't get our links working too soon, she thought.

Chapter 16

Kirizzo lurked within his enormous space fortress and spied on the Terrans thousands of kilometers below. His powerful sensor arrays allowed him to see a good part of the activity, though he couldn't see into the tunnels below the city, as they somehow blocked his scans. He believed the lower tunnels were most likely built by Trilisks. The Konuan buildings blocked some of his information, but not all. He watched both the small group allied with him and the larger group he had discovered later.

The small group was easy to observe. They had twenty scout robots that he could use to keep tabs on them even inside the surface buildings. Everywhere they went, there were always a few of the scouts nearby. The Telisa-Magnus bond remained unbroken, and in fact, Magnus refused to initiate any pairing rituals with the new Terran female. Kirizzo felt this was likely due to her age, which was at the twilight of Terran fertility.

This group's loyalty had become almost agonizing. At this point, Kirizzo hadn't invested as much as he could have in the relationship. Had he known it would last this long, he would have put more into it from the beginning. Yet doing so now seemed to be an investment doomed to fail. In a way, the longer cooperation/competition cycles Terrans used made the inevitable betrayal all the more painful. Kirizzo would have to start all over again once someone turned. And he kept putting off more investment, expecting the break to happen any time now, yet the alliance went on and on.

He had studied Terran alliances. He knew they fragmented and dissolved. Yet this one endured. What was he missing? It was almost out of a masochistic sense of morbid curiosity that he allowed it to continue.

Their initial searches hadn't uncovered anything of Trilisk origin. Kirizzo had resolved to start looking for clues from orbit. Trilisk equipment would leave clues he might be able to detect from great distances.

But instead he had discovered the large group of Terrans sharing the ruins. Their presence interested him, as the group was obviously interested in masking their presence from orbit. Kirizzo would not have been surprised to see a small settlement, but here was a group that hid by the ruins. Most likely it was another band of smugglers.

A group larger, more organized, and possibly better equipped than his current allies, it was also harder to glean information about.

Oh, the agony. Now he had a real reason to switch modes with the current Terran group. He should make an overture, investigate subtly whether or not these new smugglers might want to join him for mutual benefit.

What were the repercussions of a mistake? He had no homeworld to lose, but Telisa, Magnus, and Cilreth did know about his new base of operations and the Trilisk AI he had left there. What resources could they bring to bear against it? If they told the Terran space force about it, what might their fellow Terrans commit to recovering his treasures?

The larger group below seemed to be set up in a highly defensive posture. They had a perimeter put up, guarded by war machines and mobile sensor units on a high state of alert. This group expected trouble, or they had already experienced it. The first thing that came to mind was that they had assumed this formation upon the arrival of his sister ship holding the Terrans, but close analysis showed that the perimeter had been up for a much longer time.

There was movement in and out of the tunnels. This helped to confirm they were smugglers. That and the lack of any presence of the stagnant Terran government entity, the UNSF. These Terrans sought the same things he did— Trilisk information and technology. Kirizzo modified some search parameters. His scan picked up two interesting objects within the camp. Signatures almost certainly Trilisk. So they had already experienced some measure of success.

Kirizzo thought about other elements that might build a mutually beneficial alliance with the larger group below. In addition to the desire to obtain artifacts, their obvious lack of connections to the UNSF could be useful. Kirizzo had lost a small empire under the surface of his homeworld. His industrial seed promised the possibility of creating a new one. Should he attempt to create that new empire here, among the Terran worlds? In the open? His technological advantage carried a lot of leverage. With allies, might he hope to overthrow the UNSF and rule the Terrans himself?

The idea seemed possible. But it also sounded like a lot of work and danger for modest gain. What did the Terran civilization have that he needed? Resources, planets, yes. But knowledge? No, not really.

Kirizzo found another anomaly. Something moved down below around the group of hidden Terrans. Something with suspiciously Trilisk elements in the signature, yet it wasn't headed directly to the camp, nor were there any Terrans nearby. Was this simply a Terran carrying and operating a Trilisk trinket? Then Kirizzo considered the readings from another angle.

Could this be the reason for the perimeter?

Suddenly a big shift occurred in the lower-frequency electromagnetic environment below. It suspiciously ended at frequencies of known use to the Terrans. Was the anomaly responsible?

Kirizzo searched for the source. He pinpointed it to machines within the larger Terran perimeter. He quickly linked the electromagnetic disturbance to a new pattern of movement within their camp. Kirizzo realized it was an attack.

The group had suppressed communications likely used by other Terrans using several transmitting devices placed on high ground around the ruins. Then they had organized into armed groups, accompanied by machines of war, and set out on foot. There were many more of them than his three allies and their scout robots, but still, these smugglers were a pathetic force even by Terran military standards. It was almost as if they had scavenged their equipment or perhaps bought old surplus from the last Terran interplanetary war.

Rather than help them, he decided to test their abilities. If they were very capable, then that made them more valuable as allies. If they took losses or did not handle opposition well, it might make them more amenable to negotiation.

Kirizzo considered direct interference. His new ship possessed weapons that could disable the Terrans' surface equipment, but unfortunately the power plant providing energy for the jamming had been brought underground.

Kirizzo preferred a more indirect approach. He had analyzed and solved the mathematics of the Terran scrambler, despite the fact that it had been designed to be unpredictable by enemies. Given the ability to predict the scrambler and knowledge of the target he wanted to speak with, he could alter his own signal such that the message would get through. One-way communication became possible.

He contacted ten of the scout robots and organized them to oppose the attacking Terrans. They took up sniping positions along likely routes to the east. He left a system running to allow the scouts to coordinate with each other by sending regular messages telling them of the positions and status of all the others.

Then Kirizzo resumed his agonized decision making.

He considered the large group of Terrans again. Perhaps he should negotiate an alliance with them. On the front leg, they were organized into a clear hierarchy, meaning Kirizzo would only have to deal with the leader; he could wield the entire group with a single handle.

On the rear leg, these Terrans were organized for military purposes, meaning they were more likely to use force for their own gain. Kirizzo would have to expend more energy in protective countermeasures working with such a group. Besides, if they sought Trilisk artifacts, and already had some, that put them in competition with Kirizzo, unless they were as easily satiated with baubles as Telisa and Magnus were.

Given their advance against the scouts and his allies, Kirizzo was running out of time to decide.

Kirizzo saw a launch from the surface. Terran ships. His own ship notified him of the event. Kirizzo directed it to gather more information.

He focused in a scan. Military vessels, though out of date for the Terran space force current standards. They were multipurpose assault ships, designed to carry troops from planet to planet. They looked to be more focused on landing missions rather than space superiority weapons.

Not that it would have mattered. Kirizzo had the upper hand here. His computers analyzed the scans and found the weaknesses of the ships. He would be ready if the Terrans decided to attack without provocation. Kirizzo expected they would attempt to negotiate once they saw his ship. He allowed them to find him. Perhaps now he could enter into an agreement with the new group.

The Terran ships reached orbit. Their sluggish systems seemed to have finally located Kirizzo's vessel. The Terrans were activating weapons systems. That much, he had expected. Then they launched a wave of missiles at him.

Aggression. Kirizzo recognized it immediately, like a scoop of fresh sand in a long-stagnant cave. His decision had been made for him. He would remain allied with his current team. He started a new planning phase for the destruction of the aggressors.

Chapter 17

Arakaki put a round into her grille puncher and placed the hook around one bar of the grille in front of her. Then she placed the press plate against the wall above the opening and activated the puncher with her link. The device jumped sharply as it applied the force between the grille bar and the wall, breaking the grille free. She pulled the obstruction out with the hook then dumped it aside with a practiced motion.

Her link said that was the 1434th grille she'd pulled.

I'll take apart this entire city hunting you.

Suddenly a voice addressed her link. "Neat trick. What do you want here?"

Her link was configured to only carry messages from strangers straight through if they were in close proximity. After all, anyone that close could just speak out loud if they wanted.

Arakaki jumped to one side. Placing her back to the wall, she trained her weapon on the grill to her right. Then she drew a laser from her belt with her left hand and pointed it the other direction.

"My name is Magnus. I'm hunting an alien creature. It is very dangerous. I suggest you leave right now."

"Wheretheflip*are*you?" she said out loud.

"Shhh. I'm not coming out to get shot, if that's what you want. Are you hunting me or the Konuan?"

He must be from that ship.

"The Konuan," she replied over her link. "Are you with the space force? We saw you land."

"All you need to know is I'm hunting the Konuan and it's in this building with us. I have robots stationed around the exits."

"Those little scout robots? It's more dangerous than you think."

"Just tell me how to kill it."

143

Arakaki recognized that edge to his voice. The man who spoke to her was angry at it.

Like me.

"It's fast," she said. "It can sense us from farther away than we can sense it. Hearing, I think. It has technology, too."

"It has tech? How? These ruins—"

"Are built on top of a Trilisk outpost," Arakaki finished for him. "Now that I've given you valuable information, how about you tell me who you are?"

Magnus materialized before her. He was a soldier. Arakaki could tell that right away. He was strong, with blonde hair. He wore Momma Veer and held an older rifle in his hands. IIis rifle was pointed at her heart. She doubted her skinsuit could save her at point-blank range.

Okay, well, that rifle isn't current.

"Ex UED?" she asked quickly, hoping against hope. If he was a remnant of another unit, the out-of-date rifle would make sense. Maybe he'd had to scavenge.

"Space force, actually," he admitted slowly. "Though I'm no longer a soldier. And to be frank, no longer a friend of the world government."

Everyone still called it the *world government*, even though there were many more than one Terran-controlled world now. The words were old enough to take on meaning of their own. Politically, it was still the only world that really mattered. Other planets had large populations and healthy industries, some of which had risen up against Earth, but they hadn't been able to resist the UNSF.

Arakaki waited for hatred to come. But she only felt sad as she chomped on the tough bit of synthetic in her teeth. Of course he wasn't UED. Not in that huge new ship.

"That's a big ship you guys brought. Is it full of scientists or soldiers? Or both?"

"It's an alien ship, and we're here to find Trilisk artifacts," he said, deadpan.

Buckle bulb? No, dammit. He has to be telling the truth.

Before she could answer, he continued, "I know it's crazy, but right now we have the Konuan to worry about. You look like you can handle yourself. Stay if you want, but I'm blowing that thing to bits."

Arakaki's link added a monitoring service hosted on his link. "A hack? Why should I let you try?"

"It's the data feed from the robots I have in and around the building," he said.

Arakaki accessed the service. She saw the positions of six machines. Four waited at grilles near the entrances to the building, and two others were on a lower floor, centrally located. There was something odd about their sensor maps. They had an extra layer to the display labeled "mass map." Some kind of fancy new mass sensor suite?

He sure is trusting me quickly. Stupid bugger.

"Cross me if you want," he said, as if reading her mind. "Do it after it's dead. You must have known someone it killed. I'm a human like you, it's not even close. We get it first, okay?"

Arakaki nodded. "I'll add you to my grenade signature blacklist."

"Same here," he said. "I recognize that PAW. What's that there? Laser?"

"Yes. I don't even know what hurts the thing. But it's killed plenty of men with PAWs."

They listened for a minute, watching the feeds. Magnus knelt with his back against a column that ran from one side of the floor vent to the ceiling vent. Arakaki did the same, facing another direction.

"These buildings are tricky," Arakaki said. "You can see through half the building in any direction through these grilles, yet any room could have an ambusher waiting in a corner out of sight."

"I have to search. I lost a friend," Magnus said. She could hear it was true. "She's tough. Got a lot of tricks up her sleeve. There's a chance she's not dead. So I have to go looking."

"It'll kill you for sure," Arakaki said. "It knows you want to find your friend. It'll wait for you."

"Stay here. Or help search. Up to you," he said.

He's not going to abandon his friend. Stupid, yet admirable. "Which way first?"

"Crawl through that vent. Then we head that way. We can cover each other a bit," he suggested.

"The best we could hope for is one of us shoots the thing while it eats the head off the other," Arakaki said coldly.

"You're familiar with it, then," Magnus said. "All I know is what you told me. It's fast, and a hit-and-run type of creature. Has tech. Good hearing. Likes to attack the head." The man's Veer head guard came up across the back of his head.

"It's a Konuan, like you said. They were nasty things, fast, thin, like umbrella-shaped bats that can hang from the ceiling. When they open up, they can almost completely cover you then snap back shut. Then digest you with acid spit or venom."

Arakaki moved slowly. She didn't plan to shoot Magnus, at least not yet, but he was still watching her.

And with good reason. I have two deadly weapons and I'm UED. But he wants his friend and he knows I can help. Or die trying.

"Acid. I guess that makes it easier to dine on any creature made of carbon, hydrogen, and oxygen no matter what planet it's from," Magnus said.

"I think it just does it to kill us. Look, I was serious when I said the best we can hope for is for one of us to kill it when it kills the other one of us. I suggest stay in sight of each other. If I point my weapon at you, just duck."

Magnus nodded. "Then I have an idea," he said. "But I doubt you'll like it much."

***

Telisa heard breathing. To her heightened hearing, the act involved a dozen vortices of air, slurping past lips, tongue, and throat, and sliding around bronchial tubes and the internal flexible sacs of human lungs. It was a complex, wet sound.

It's Magnus. I can tell just by hearing him breathe. I've heard hints of this a million times before: listening to him exercise, sleep, and make love. There is so much more to his breathing now, but I can recognize it. I just know it's him, even from fifty meters away through these cramped cubes and ventways. Amazing!

Someone else. Was it Cilreth? No. It didn't seem right.

I can hear her. I know it's a woman. But I can't picture it as Cilreth. Too…small, too compact. Too strong. Cilreth is taller, older, slower.

Telisa was amazed at how rich an information source her hearing could be. So many details beyond what human hearing could deliver to her. She could tell how large the Terrans were, and she could hear the echoes of their movements all around, telling her where the rooms and the grilles were. The building seemed like so much more now…in fact, she realized part of its design was about carrying sound through the building by lining up the grilles in each direction. Crawling to the middle of the room let you know what was happening in the entire area, but moving off to a corner made it milder, more distant. She moved to the center of the room and listened more.

Telisa heard the scraping of tiny claws across stone.

It's the other one! Here in this building. Maybe Magnus can kill it! But he wants to kill me, too.

"It's in this building," she heard Magnus say. His voice resonated with a hundred details Telisa had never heard before.

"Yes," the female voice replied. "I have a mobile sensor suite parked outside. But don't think we've trapped it here. It's just playing with us."

"Here we go," Magnus said. Then he stopped breathing.

Here we go? Go where? What happened?

Telisa only heard the noises of the woman's movement. She prepared the tool she had to pry out the next vent. Telisa tensed. That tool was unpleasantly abrupt and noisy. She shuffled toward the nearest corner. Still there was no sign of Magnus, as if he had disappeared.

Of course. He turned on the stealth sphere. He's still there. She's the bait.

The thunderclap came and went. Telisa felt relief it was over.

If they shoot their weapons, that sound might hurt, too. Five Entities! A stunner is a sonic weapon. It would be unbelievably loud to me.

The instant Telisa realized a stunner would be formidable to a Konuan, she knew what she wanted to do.

I have to tell Magnus a stunner might incapacitate a Konuan. Might incapacitate me.

The awful sound of the grille breaker snapped through the building. Telisa ignored it. She moved out onto the wall two meters above the floor.

She moved her legs carefully, scraping the wall for long moments, though she worked as fast as she could.

The other will hear me clearly. Is the other my enemy right now? Will it seek me out?

She heard the scraping again. It was moving around the far side of them. Coming at them from behind, through the doors they had forced open.

No! Magnus, look out!

Telisa felt the thrill of the Konuan danger response: nervous legs, razor-sharp hearing, and a chemical stimulant released from a thousand tiny pouches under her outer integument. She could feel her skin tightening.

Without my link how can I warn him? He thinks we're both dangerous! But he's on my trail. That's exactly what the other Konuan wants. It will kill him.

Michael McCloskey

Chapter 18

Cilreth stared at the pillars. All three opened at her command, but none seemed to hold Telisa inside. There was only the pile of green remains she thought must be a dead Trilisk.

Trilisk devices can hear and understand my thoughts. Not through my link. Just by an unobtrusive scan. I wonder how it is I have permission to use anything.

She stood in the center of the room, stymied. "I need a list of services," she thought aloud. "Possibilities." Her gaze fell on the green thing in the tube. She had been avoiding it, so unpleasant was its appearance and meaning. It was even uglier than the giant lobster thing that had tried to kill her.

If that's a Trilisk body, then maybe it has a Trilisk link in it.

She walked over to the tube. She thought about how amazing a Trilisk link must be. If she had one with her, if she could use it, maybe she could use Trilisk machines from the ruins wherever she went. It could be a game-changer.

This is crazy.

She asked the inner tube to open. The clear material slid away just as the outer shell of the column had. Cilreth watched with growing discomfort. She waited for a bad smell. There was none. The fuzz-covered corpse sagged further as the clear barrier slipped down into the floor. Cilreth dropped to her knees next to it.

Then she began to probe through the corpse. She took out anything from her pack that might help her. A water locator and purifier. A poison detector. She looked at the remains in several wavelengths through her laser scope. Nothing she had was designed to look through an alien body. She found a medical device in her pack. One of the things it could do was locate foreign objects lodged in a

Terran body. She tried it on the corpse. It showed a hundred things inside the body it thought were problems: everything from shrapnel to parasites.

Okay, that thing is obviously whacked out since it's not looking into a human.

"Nothing left but to dig in," she said to herself. She held an eating fork and knife and stared down at the pile. "Ugh. Ugh. I can't do this," she said out loud.

She thought again about the link. If she dug through a human body, it would take a while, but she would eventually find the link. Would the same hold for this alien corpse?

Trilisks were so advanced they probably didn't need links. If they had them, they might have been the size of a single cell. Or all their machines read their minds, just like my link does with me, from the outside. And plants thoughts and information right back into the brain without any device?

Cilreth sneezed.

"Great, now I have some awful space disease," she said, not really believing it. She looked at the pile of green fuzz again. "But what if you went on a trip? You didn't have a link to bring with you? Internal helpers, protectors, power sources?"

Cilreth closed her eyes. *Where is the link? Where is the link?*

She opened her eyes. The display across the room had changed. It showed a three-armed, three-legged creature. Like the robot they had found, it was deep blue, almost crystalline. She saw subtle differences. This body was a bit rounder, softer. The body became transparent. Within the volume of the body, complex lines began to form. They crisscrossed the body space like a nervous system. Several spots around the body pulsed with more light. Some of them expanded as she looked at them, close-ups of more complicated webs within.

"The entire body is integrated like a link. Or at least the entire nervous system," she said slowly. "So there's my answer."

Cilreth dug a sample cylinder out of her pack. She looked down at the remains and scooped some into the container. Then she threw it back out. She looked at the display and concentrated on one of the most complex areas. It magnified to show more detail.

"Where? Where is that part here?"

She looked down. Part of the body glowed. She could see through it.

Cilreth reached down and carefully scooped up her sample to include the parts displayed.

"Gruesome, but effective," she said to herself. "I have something here. Something I hope isn't too scrambled to be analyzed."

Cilreth scanned the room again. She didn't see any threats, but she realized she had not been paying enough attention to notice. The Vovokan spheres were watching her, at least. They rotated lazily around the tube she had dug in.

"Where's Telisa?" she asked again.

The other column displayed the flat creature. Cilreth felt only frustration. She took a deep breath and approached the display.

"No. This. I want her," she thought, bringing up the image of Telisa in her mind. "Where?"

A pane opened in her PV. The routing protocol was accessed and a route entered into her link. Cilreth accessed the map. There was a display of more tunnels she had not been in yet. And a red line marked a path through them.

"She's there?" Cilreth asked. Nothing happened. "Then that's where I need to be," she said. Cilreth opened her eyes. The display before her showed a Terran brain again.

The brain was utterly dark. Devoid of all activity.

Oh no. She isn't dead, is she?

Cilreth stuffed the sample tube in her pack and hefted her laser rifle. She followed the map out a tunnel across from where she had entered.

Chapter 19

"I heard a grenade go off at the entrance, but my machine there is still intact," Magnus said.

"I got a close miss on the Konuan with a grenade," Arakaki replied.

"Has it been hurt? Maybe we can track it now."

"Don't think it for a second. It will use the blood trail to lead us into a trap," Arakaki said over her link. "If it even has blood. Besides, it was an incendiary."

"We have a trap of our own," Magnus transmitted back. "And the scout robots."

"Better than nothing. The bugs aren't even worth mentioning."

"The bugs—my scouts—are of limited use, but if I have one train its laser right at a grille, it could shoot fast. No target sig. Just if it moves, fry it. The machine has a destructive discharge option. And they can sense moving mass through walls. An alien trick. They can see it coming, I guarantee it." *Unless it has a Trilisk trick to defeat that. I gotta be more careful what I guarantee these days.*

Magnus meant the scout could blow its entire energy supply in one shot, which would damage or destroy the laser, but the strike would probably vaporize anything short of a tank. Which should be good enough to fry one Konuan; super fast or not, it wasn't faster than light. Or more accurately, faster than the ramp-up speed of the laser delivery system, which was very fast.

"Then it will shoot us if we get in the fire corridor," Arakaki replied.

"The scouts will be at an angle. I won't put them right in front of the grille. They can stay in corners and cover the grille opening. The center position is for us."

"Good luck picking the grille," Arakaki said.

"They have mass sensors, remember? And the other one has a glue grenade launcher. And these grilles are small. One shot for each one and they're blocked off..."

Arakaki gave him a new look.

She realizes I may have a plan forming here.

"Okay, that's good," she said. "We can block off the tunnel entrance at the bottom of the building with a couple of armed grenades. If it drops down there, boom. The scouts can glue off the exit routes..."

"Except one."

"Yes. Except one."

"That traps it in here with us," Magnus said.

"No, that pretty much traps us in here with it. We're toast, my friend. Or my enemy, or whatever the hell you are." She paused. "It's still around. I'm getting a few readings of it nearby," Arakaki took out two grenades. Magnus caught sight of a flash of green from them; then she dropped them to the ground. They spun off.

"It's staying here with us," Magnus said. He told his scouts to glue the grilles shut by the exits. He wanted to restrict the movements of the Konuan, give him a chance at a clear shot.

Arakaki shifted but didn't flinch when she heard the sounds of the glue capsules popping through the building.

"We should move to cover these two exit grilles I busted open," he said, showing her a map through his link.

"Gluing us in? I doubt it's concerned."

"Well, it should be," Magnus said.

Arakaki kept out both the UED PAW and her laser. Her weapons were shorter range, but fast to aim and rapid firing. Magnus felt reassured by the familiar feel of his old rifle, even if it wasn't as optimal for a fight in the tight confines of the building.

"It's nearby. Coming closer," she said.

"Which way? How do you know?" Magnus replied over his link.

In reply, Arakaki sent him a pointer to a feed. It opened in his PV. He saw information from the sensor module outside. In response, he gave her access to his own sight and his weapon's scan feed through his link. It was trusting her with a great deal, but Magnus was in grave danger anyway, and he felt like trusting her was a solid gamble.

A moment later her sight feed joined the channel. Magnus looked it over along with the sensor data.

"I see two sigs here," Magnus transmitted.

"Never. There's never been two. It's messing with us," Arakaki said. "One is fake. Or both."

He heard the hiss of a laser. He had missed whatever it was she saw. "You saw it?"

"My laser did."

"You have it on auto?"

"The only way to be fast enough," she said.

"Send me your target sig."

Her weapon sent his rifle a target profile. It was a lot more detailed than he had put together so far, so he loaded it and told his weapon to shoot as soon as it saw that signature again.

Then he caught sight of the creature on the mass sensor of a scout.

"There, by the north exit," he said. It was probably trying to dig through the farthest grille, the one the scout had plugged up with glue. It darted away quickly and dropped off the mass map.

"Cover me," he sent. The he realized it would be hard to cover an invisible person. In fact, to try might simply get him shot. "Scratch that."

"I know I said we should stick together but…I'm wired to explode if that damn thing burns my head off," she said.

Magnus paused. *She's serious.*

157

"Okay," he said, since he didn't know what else to say. "Thanks for the heads-up." *No pun intended.*

He crouched and entered an adjacent room filled with old garbage, scraps of iron, and what looked like a long, low table with dozens of legs. Something caught his eye, but it wasn't a Konuan.

A single word had been scraped onto the wall: "stunner." Magnus kept his weapon trained down the new corridor of grille holes toward a glued dead-end.

Stunner? Why would it say that? How did it know? I don't even know what it means even though it's readable. And I don't have a stunner. Telisa. Maybe she wrote that after getting separated from Cilreth? Maybe she's still alive.

"The wall says 'stunner' in here. Nothing else. Just that word," he said. Before Arakaki could reply, his rifle saw a long creature flit through the air in the room ahead. It matched its signature close enough that the weapon took the shot. The weapon thundered twice. A smart round registered hits on its logged target less than a second later.

"Got it!"

***

Painfully loud pops echoed through the building. Telisa reeled from the input. It took her a moment to clear her mind and identify them: glue grenade detonations.

Magnus is gluing us in here together. With the other one.

A funny scraping sound—no, two sounds—scuttled along through nearby rooms then headed down to the tunnel entrance at the bottom of the building. Something fast and loud.

The native creatures are very quiet. Magnus must have sent some devices down to the tunnel below...grenades?

Telisa could intermittently hear the other Konuan. Sometimes it scurried through one or two rooms; other times it remained still, just breathing. She decided to follow it around the outside rooms. When it struck, maybe she could intervene, somehow.

Is it trying to escape? I doubt it. It's lurking on the perimeter waiting to go in and kill them. This is life or death. I can't let my shock at this situation hold me back any longer. I have to do something.

Telisa found her courage. She didn't really know her new body, but she knew she had to try something. She couldn't let Magnus die. And if she died trying to save him, well, she didn't really want to live the rest of her life as a flat crawler anyway. Not even an acute-hearing, swift-jumping crawler. She felt on edge.

More of that carpet-creature adrenaline.

She shuffled toward the other Konuan more rapidly. She flitted across a room to the far wall, then crawled into the same room as the other. She didn't need to spot it with her antennae lights; she could hear exactly where it was. She jumped toward it. Her body was a jumble of nerves.

It launched itself before she arrived. She landed directly in its spot. She didn't feel like lingering there, so she jumped again on a parallel course.

A jet of acid sprayed the wall where she'd been a split second earlier. The substance fizzled on the wall, emitting a foul odor.

That would have hurt. How can I do that?

Telisa thought of spitting. She felt two muscular cylinders at the front edge of her body tense.

I think maybe I can spit back.

But the other Konuan had already jumped again. She landed, then launched after it. She spit at it in midair, launching a stream of her own. Then something shot past her, hurting her. The edge of her body had been clipped. A loud boom ripped through the room, then another.

Someone shot me!

Telisa felt something vaguely like pain. Her mind rang with the sensory overload of the loud noises. She wondered how bad the wound was. She landed on acid. The bite of it came through her legs, and something in her undersides reacted sharply. She jumped away before she had a chance to think it over.

It skips by, I follow it, and Magnus and that woman are slower than us, so they end up shooting at me. They don't even realize I'm following it.

The other Konuan shot off into the next room. Telisa hid behind a metal machine attached to the ceiling. It looked like it could be anything from an old printing press to a laundry steamer. There was a handle that could press two flat plates together. She hid under them both.

If I make noise now, it will just distract them from it. And if I keep chasing it, I'll just get shot more. I should be smarter.

She had to think carefully to even distinguish between the ceiling, walls, and floor. She flitted over toward a wall. There she scratched another message: "two konuan."

Then she pursued the other again. It was lurking only one room away from the woman. Telisa darted into the same room with it again. In a flash, she spit acid and leaped toward it. Only in flight did she realize she would land in her own acid. But she had sprayed it across a wide area this time, trying to make sure she at least grazed the target.

The other leaped away. A few droplets struck it as it headed away. Telisa could not alter her own course much in midair, but she tried.

A huge noise boomed over them. It made Telisa's body shake. But it was worse for the other: a chunk of its hide flew off with a round that punched through the corner of its body.

***

The creature is toying with us.

Magnus felt waste heat in his weapon from the rounds he'd fired. One of his bullets had reported a hit before disintegrating on a wall. Arakaki's laser hissed, but Magnus didn't stop to wonder if it had hit.

He slipped the last grenade off his belt and armed it with the Konuan signature. It took him one more second to make sure it wouldn't detonate near Arakaki, since she wasn't on his predesignated safe list. Then the grenade whizzed off, bouncing along the ground like a tire that had flown off a dune buggy at high speed. It bounded straight through a grille into an adjacent chamber.

Magnus reacquired the blocked grille on his rifle and waited. If it tried to escape the grenade, it might fly into his vision again. He waited for two breaths; then the grenade flew into the far room, little more than a streak of black. Magnus narrowed his eyes.

The grenade exploded, sending flashes of white flame blasting through the ruined grille. The device had reported an imminent hit before detonation.

Got it! I think.

***

Her hearing had been damaged. Yet she could still hear the Terran approaching as if she had bells and whistles attached to her. Then she heard Magnus again. He must have turned off the stealth sphere. She easily picked up the sound of their clothing rubbing as they moved and the crunch of their feet on the dusty floor. Two of them now. Magnus and the other one. The odd pain feeling had returned and intensified, along with the confusing shock of loud noise. Her body did not respond to her.

I have to move again, I have to get out of here…

The pain was so severe she almost changed her mind and wished for death. On queue, Death slipped into the room. The woman with the laser and the carbine. The laser was pointed right at Telisa. Her Konuan body trembled. She was not sure she could jump again. At least not in a way she could land on her feet like before.

Then Magnus walked through. He looked at the other woman for a moment, then trained his own weapon at Telisa.

No, Magnus, it's me, it's me…

Her legs started to scratch out a message. They opened fire.

Chapter 20

Holtzclaw couldn't reach most of his own men by link, and he hadn't been able to get an update on the assault in orbit, either. The squads that had moved out had been able to daisy chain their communications when the jamming had turned against them, but nothing outside his assault group could be reached. That included the Hellrakers.

"Sir, take a look to the east," a member of his squad transmitted. Holtzclaw turned in his powered suit to take a look.

Black clouds of smoke rose into the sky behind them. So the camp had been hit, too. Just minutes ago a flurry of fire had come in, seemingly from all directions. Some of the Guardians had been taken out by guided missiles. Holtzclaw's own squad still had their Guardian, though he half expected it to blow up at any moment.

This may be our last battle. This must have been UNSF after all, or at least a well-armed expedition.

"Stay in range of each other. Time to strike back. Remember, we still outnumber them. Likely they just blew their entire ordinance supply on our base," Holtzclaw told his men. Of course, it was pure speculation. Highly optimistic speculation.

He left his cover and resumed the advance. His squad joined him. They rose from behind rocks, through plant patches, and emerged from niches between the ruined buildings. The Guardian machine resumed its march, adding the sound of moving machinery to the march.

Kowalewski sent him a private message.

"Arakaki's out there. She's wasn't synced up to cut through the jammers while we had them up, and now I can't reach her anyway."

"She's a good survivor," Holtzclaw said. "She's on our friendly list, and that's going to have to be enough." He double-checked his weapon's settings and verified all his men were in it. The list was considerably shorter than it had been when he stepped up as a colonel.

"Split up. Kowalewski leads five squads to their big ship. We have to take it. I'm with the rest of us going into the ruins after the scientists we saw. We'll need to secure their cooperation, maybe even use them as hostages. So set your weapons to wound."

Their PAWs and the projectiles they used could distinguish friend from foe with fair accuracy, and the rounds could veer in flight to strike things matching their target signatures. That included the ability to turn some percentage of lethal hits into disabling ones. Holtzclaw checked his men's weapons through his link. They had all obeyed his orders.

The battle group split. There were now two missions. Holtzclaw's squads turned south and moved through the ruins at a good clip. The city looked the same as it did on any other day—a maze of old buildings and alien plants. The sky remained as clear as always. It rarely rained, and when it did, all the water drained into the fissures where the plants rooted themselves.

Holtzclaw picked up information from another probe. He checked its history while his hand found its way to his shoulder to scrape off more old skin. Arakaki! She had taken it into the ruins after the monster. And there had been non-UED Terrans within its range.

"We have a friendly in the area," Holtzclaw reminded his three squads. It was easy to forget things like that when the fighting started. "Arakaki. She was after the monster."

"I hope she got it, sir," Schimke said.

Holtzclaw knew between the monster and the scientists she might have had her hands full.

If anyone comes out of this alive, she will, he thought.

"We have to find these scientists or whatever they are. They may be key to getting what we need from the ship. These three buildings first," Holtzclaw said, showing the men his map. "Each squad take one and work your way down to the tunnels below. Most likely that's what they came to investigate. Arakaki may well have found her way to the tunnels as well, if she was hunting the Konuan. Report any signs of recent activity so we can close in on them."

Holtzclaw and his officers had long suspected the Trilisk tunnels were heavily used by the monster to move about the city without being detected. They had set a few traps down there, but somehow the thing that hunted them never fell for it.

The squads approached the buildings Holtzclaw had indicated. His personal squad's Guardian covered them as they moved forward to find new spots next to buildings or in depressions in the rock. Then the Guardian machine moved forward. Holtzclaw caught sight of the probe, stationed outside one of the buildings he'd targeted.

Holtzclaw told his Guardian to patrol the vicinity of the buildings on the surface. It would never fit into the tight Konuan warrens. He configured it to fire low, at the feet of any Terrans it did not recognize. Its projectiles were so powerful, even striking the rocks below a running person would likely cause pieces of the sharp red rock to fly up and wound the target.

His squad had just reached the building and sent in a couple of grenades when combat broke out at one of the other buildings. Holtzclaw heard distant shots fired.

"We're taking fire! Light so far. We definitely have some of them holed up in here," came the message from his second squad leader.

Holtzclaw's squad looked to him. He checked the tunnel map. As expected, the two buildings linked up.

"Pressure them from topside," Holtzclaw told the second squad leader. "We'll come in from below in the tunnel from the west. If we hurry we might trap them in there."

Then to his own squad: "Double-time it! Through the building! Find the well room and get into that tunnel!"

Chapter 21

Telisa awakened.

Not again! Crap.

She drew in a long breath. In fact, the breath continued flowing in, in, in for a long time, until her chest had expanded like a giant balloon.

Chest? I have lungs. Big lungs.

She moved an arm. An immensely huge, strong arm that extended so very far.

Wait. Wait. This is different, but it's good different. Human different?

She saw only darkness. Her hearing felt muted. Normal, lame Terran hearing. She felt around in the dark. Was it her own body?

Female. I'm female…

She felt a tiny ridge of a scar on her wrist where a Vovokan nasty had sampled her. And her hair was the right length.

I think I'm me! And my link?

An army of view panes exploded in her mind's eye. Her link offered her its many services.

"Anyone there?" she asked tentatively through her link.

"Telisa?" The reply was marked as coming from Cilreth.

"Yes! Where in the hell am I?"

"Stay calm. I think you're…I think you're in a Trilisk column."

"Please get me out." Telisa asked it in a calm way, but the panic was only just below the surface. Her recent experiences had all been too much.

"Then just think it: open. Think you want it open. Pray to it."

"There's a prayer device?" she said. Without waiting for an answer, she thought: *I want out. Please open!*

At first there was only a humming sound. Then a growing sliver of light appeared above her. It widened until she could see that some kind of sheath over the tube was dropping down from the top. In a few seconds she would be free!

"It's opening!" Telisa said. "Wait. I'm still inside some kind of clear tube."

"It takes longer," Cilreth said calmly. Her friend's voice reassured her. "Telisa, can you hear me?"

"Oh, thank the Five," Telisa croaked.

"It's okay now. Let's get you out of there."

"Cilreth. You're not going to believe where I've been! Magnus just killed me!"

"Maybe you'd better just rest for a minute and take some deep breaths."

She think's I'm delusional. Lack of oxygen?

"It's a Trilisk body switcher," Telisa explained.

"That's not possible."

"Think about it, Cilreth. This is Trilisk stuff we're clowning around with."

"Your brain is trained throughout your infancy to grow and adapt its connections and signals from your own—"

"Yes, I know. Believe me, I know. But sufficiently advanced technology can adapt my personality and thought patterns onto other nervous systems and map my body signals to those of radically different creatures." Telisa stood up carefully.

"It would be much more complicated than a simple mapping unless the target creature was totally humanoid." But now her voice carried less conviction. Cilreth was thinking on it.

"I know. I know. Yet it only took a bit of practice. I was one of the slugs. The Konuan were a lot cooler than stupid slugs, by the way. Just ask Magnus when he gets back. He killed me."

He must think I'm dead. Even if he doesn't know that was me.

"What?" Cilreth asked.

"I'm going to have to give him a hard time for that."

"You really believe all that happened? It was probably virtual," Cilreth said.

Telisa nodded. She didn't believe it had been imaginary at all, but she didn't blame Cilreth for thinking it. It was more logical to assume such adventures had occurred in a simulation.

It was just that Telisa knew the Trilisks could do it.

A tremor rumbled through the tunnels. Telisa felt her body shake. Her legs still felt just a bit long. Her head was so far from the ground. She bent her knees to compensate for a sudden lack of confidence in her ability to balance herself.

"Uh oh," Cilreth summed up. "Are you okay?"

"I'm still adapting to my new body," she said. Cilreth's face reflected the oddity of Telisa's statement. Then she got a link connection from Magnus.

"Telisa?"

"Magnus! Where are you?"

"The building where you got separated from Cilreth," he said. "I'm coming toward you."

"Oh! I guess our links are working again then," she said. "Who is that woman you're with?" Telisa's voice sounded a bit more accusatory than she intended. But her demand had a lot of emotional charge to it.

"What? How do you know about her?"

"Long story. Is she an explorer?"

"She's UED. She took off. I'm not sure we can count her as a friend."

"What? They're here?"

"Cilreth didn't tell you? Are you with her?"

"Yes. She didn't say anything yet...she hasn't had a chance, I guess." Telisa said out loud to Cilreth, "I'm in touch with Magnus."

"Me too," Cilreth said.

"I heard an explosion," Telisa said. "Well, felt one, anyway."

"It wasn't the *Clacker*," Magnus told them.

"I can't believe the UED still exists. What can we do?"

"We have to stay in the buildings and tunnels. Anything on the surface is a sitting duck. They can kill us from kilometers away with a standard artillery system and a basic detection grid, which they have to have set up. I saw some combat machines. Nothing frontline, but maybe they have more than I saw. There's no way you could get out unless you use Cilreth's stealth suit."

"We'll wait for you," Telisa said.

"Prepare yourself. We may have to surrender. We can't fight robots. And there may be hundreds of them."

"I have the breaker claw," she mentioned.

"What's its range? I doubt your reflexes can compete with military hardware. Good news is they may want us alive to get them the *Clacker*. They must wonder what the hell it is."

"That's good news? That just means we're about to be captured and tortured," said Cilreth.

Telisa looked around the room. Three tunnels led out in different directions. One of the three huge pillars had opened to emit her. The room looked empty otherwise, though she suspected the other pillars and maybe the walls were full of surprises.

"You two could use your stealth to leave and get back to the *Clacker*," Telisa said.

"No. What would you do?" Cilreth said.

"I could...hide in the tube again."

"They would find you eventually. Or you might suffocate in there."

"I don't think so," Telisa said. "Maybe I could even become Konuan again. Fight them that way."

"Out of the question," said Magnus. Telisa turned and saw him entering from one of the connecting passageways. She walked over and embraced him.

Thank the Five we're back together.

Even with the UED moving in, something about his physical presence steadied her.

"These tunnels are long and straight. They'll be able to overwhelm us easily here. We need to move up into a building and dig in. Those tiny cubic rooms have a lot of vents, but they have a lot of corners, too. We might be able to stand them off for a while. The fact our links operate again means Shiny has been working some magic. Maybe he can rescue us."

"That scaredy cat? He probably left," Cilreth said.

"I doubt it," Telisa said. "He's got our back."

Michael McCloskey

Chapter 22

Within the Gorgalan ship far above Chigran Callnir Four, a golden creature with forty legs burst into a room. It sent a signal to a large walking machine, causing a cockpit atop the machine to open. Kirizzo marched inside and curled up within the tight confines. He didn't hesitate. His planning phase had finished while aboard the spaceship high above the planet. He activated the walker. The shining metal machine lifted on its eight slender legs and walked into another spacious chamber. A bay door slid open to accept the machine. Anchor tentacles slid out to secure the machine within the small bay.

Then the part of the starship holding the walker detached and dropped toward the planet, taking Kirizzo with it. He watched the events piped into his long, thin brain from sensors outside the drop module. The planet's surface below expanded to take over more of his field of vision. The drop module descended unerringly toward the ruined Konuan city.

An invisible beam of concentrated energy lanced out of the sky. Kirizzo saw it only with the help of his drop module's sensor array. His vision magnified the target far below. A black cloud of smoke rose up as he descended on the ruins. Kirizzo took note of the hit. The Terran artillery machine had been destroyed by fire from his ship. In all likelihood the other artillery robots would quickly share the same fate.

Kirizzo watched many sources of data, among them a video feed from the *Clacker*. It showed an object in the sky growing from a distant silver dot to the size of a small house as it dropped onto the surface. A battle walker burst from the belly of the drop module, hitting the ground running.

From his position nestled inside the walker, Kirizzo issued a series of rapid commands with mental impulses.

Tiny spherical drones dropped out of the machine and flew in all directions. The drones would be able to block incoming fire from the Terrans.

Kirizzo's scan told him dozens of Terrans had advanced across the ruins toward the *Clacker*. No doubt the alien ship was their primary objective.

The spider-legged walking machine clambered over the sharp red rocks toward the UED base. The Terran soldiers were deployed directly in his path. To get even more details about their disposition, he contacted the *Clacker* and told the ship to launch two reconnaissance drones to scan the landscape from low altitude. Between those drones, the ship in orbit, and the *Clacker*, Kirizzo should have total information about the battlefield. It was also enough to give his information net some redundancy should some of his machines be destroyed.

Projectiles started to strike the walker. Portions of the power reserve were expended to hold the outer surface in place as the kinetic energy of the rounds slammed into it. The walker hunkered down on its legs, making itself harder to spot.

Six attack drones shot from the belly of the walker. They hurtled away, gaining altitude as they left. Meanwhile more large projectiles rained toward the swerving walker. One struck the outer surface of the machine in a vulnerable spot. The energy reserve wasn't sufficient to defend against the round, so it damaged the outer skin of Kirizzo's machine. The walker rotated, carrying the damaged area away from the line of fire until it could be repaired.

The attack drones arrived at the Terran line and selected the large robots that fired upon the walker. The flying spheres each split into six pieces and accelerated further. Within the next second, several of the attack machines and a dozen of the Terran soldiers were obliterated.

The other nearby Terran squads had taken cover. The walker shot ten seeker bullets into the sky. The guided projectiles started to patrol. One by one, they spotted enemies below and dove down, going supersonic as they accelerated toward their targets. Each one killed a Terran, easily punching through the light battle suits then exploding. Terran body parts started to rain across the landscape.

But Kirizzo was not paying much attention to the devastation he visited upon the faction of Terrans in competition with him. He could have disabled that force from orbit if it had been his only goal. He was focused on the anomalous life form he had tracked across the surface.

He suspected it might be a Trilisk.

The creature of interest had disappeared underground within a minute of his arrival on the surface. Kirizzo decided to enlist the aid of his allies to track the anomaly.

"Team. Enemy not pursuing."

"Not pursuing you or me?" Telisa replied.

"However, target of intense interest spotted in ruins," Kirizzo said. "Prepare to assist with capture of possible Trilisk in lower tunnel system."

There was a delay.

"It's good to hear you, Shiny," Telisa replied. "We're fighting for our lives, will assist if you get us out of this."

Kirizzo reviewed his status information of the Terrans on his side. He located their signals within a building. Several clues indicated they had been engaged. Kirizzo altered the course of his walker toward the building. The machine made good time, walking over the uneven rocks gracefully, dodging around patches of vegetation and even clambering right over the lowest Konuan buildings.

Occasional Terran small-arms fire zinged by the walker or bounced off its surface. Kirizzo ignored it until larger, more significant projectiles clanged against his machine, affecting the energy reserves. Another Terran fighting machine had acquired him. His drones accelerated to intervene. Automated systems returned fire, sending out four seeker rounds to counter the attacker.

The rounds slammed into the machine and detonated. The flimsy machine exploded. Metal parts flew in all directions. His drones veered away, seeking other targets.

"Battle machine outside shelter neutralized," Kirizzo reported. His walker showed him the attacking Terrans within the building. They were split into groups to surround his allies. "Enemies moving in to flank, trap, surprise you from below."

"Below us? Which direction are you? Should we make a run for it?"

Shiny analyzed the disposition of enemies in the alien construct.

"Proceed south. Will cover retreat, withdrawal, emergence from building."

Chapter 23

A round smacked against the floor next to Magnus. He felt the sting of a tiny fragment of hot metal impacting his cheek. His attendant spheres had stopped orbiting. Now they darted back and forth in front of the grille he faced prone.

If that round had another meter to arc toward me, I'd be very dead.

But it meant his position was about right. He had taken a position just far enough to the side of the fire corridor through the grille opening that the incoming projectiles couldn't alter their course sharply enough to hit him. Though he had cut it a bit closer than intended. In fact, the attendant drones seemed to be oblivious to the limitation of the incoming rounds, and they tended to intercept them anyway, which sent shrapnel flying. He considered overriding them but decided he was not *that* confident a round would not hit him.

"We're going to be split by this grille corridor as soon as they make it in here, and if they get to either side we'll be pinned. Then the grenades will come," Telisa said.

Magnus smiled. *She knows a hell of a lot more than when I met her.* "Don't forget you and Cilreth have stealth options. You can cross over these grill corridors if you time it right. You have your attendants? I don't think their assault robots will fit in here."

Though they might be able to just blow through the walls. I wonder if they're low on supplies.

"I lost one sphere in the tunnels," Telisa said. That made Magnus frown. Shiny had given them each two for good reason. The alien himself had five or six at all times since he resupplied upon returning from Thespera.

The grille corridors created long fire lanes by the way the grilles lined up in each direction through the building: roughly east/west, north/south, and to a lesser degree, even up/down. Magnus armed his last grenade and sent it out toward the entrance they had used. Most likely the UED forces would open all the outer grilles.

"I could go find a tube and try to become Konuan again," Telisa transmitted. "I bet I would be able to take some of them out, maybe do some hit and run. And if they mistake me for the one that's been hunting here for a long time, they might break and leave."

"I don't want to be separated again," Cilreth said. She activated her stealth suit. "I'll scout another way out. Pull a grille or two if I have to."

"No. You're better off dug in here with us," Magnus said. "I have an edge. I have still access to a UED sensor module. I can see most of them."

He didn't mention that he could see they were very outnumbered. But they had the defender's advantage, good cover, and a few high-tech tricks to pull.

Telisa seemed to accept his opinion.

We just survived one close call, and now we're about to die all over again. We were supposed to be better prepared this time.

His grenade detonated on an enemy grenade in an empty room before them.

"They're coming," Magnus said. He watched the enemy in his link along with the views from his team and the attendant spheres. "One squad is covering them, and another has moved forward, just three chambers ahead of us."

Cilreth and Telisa exchanged looks. Telisa put her smart pistol back at her belt and took out the prize weapon from Shiny's vault: her chain lightning gun.

"Don't move," she sent Cilreth and Magnus. She moved to the side of the advancing enemy, into an adjacent room. Magnus saw the UED forces were already moving to flank them on both sides of the building.

Damn, those grille pullers of theirs work fast.

Magnus rolled into the fire corridor and fired twice just to give someone something to think about. Somehow the attendant spheres knew to leave outgoing fire alone. He immediately rolled back to his previous spot. The feed from the probe showed he was getting some response. But what would likely happen next was going to be unpleasant. He expected a return volley from a heavy weapon, a round of grenades, or worse.

But the enemy decided to play it patient and wait for the flanking maneuver to complete.

Is that more evidence they want us alive? Or just low ammunition? Do they overestimate us?

Telisa disappeared from Magnus's natural sight, but he watched the feed from her eyes: she moved up to the grille opening and rested the heavy body of the weapon in the center of it. Every second she sat there she risked a smart round flying through and nailing her in the forehead. Her attendant sphere darted back and forth between three grill openings fitfully. It actually looked agitated. Fear for her life gripped Magnus, yet he said nothing. She was doing what had to be done. Fortunately the moment passed when she activated the alien weapon.

A bright flash of light burned his retinas. For the next second the only thing that really registered was a vague impression of Telisa rolling away to the corner to get back to safety.

Thunder rolled through the building; then everything became quiet. That, or his ears were damaged. His Veer suit's diagnostic reported its ear-protection dampening system was working. Magnus checked the probe data. The connection had dropped, and it refused to come back.

"Magnus? Cilreth? Are you alive?" Telisa asked quickly.

"Yes. I'm still here. In one piece, I think," Cilreth said.

179

"I'm alive," Magnus said. "You took a lot of them out. But you must have also destroyed the sensor I was using, because I'm not getting data from it anymore."

"What now? Will more of them come?" asked Cilreth.

"Maybe you could take a peek," Telisa said. "You and Magnus."

Magnus realized she meant he still had the stealth sphere. Sheepishly, he rolled it over to her across the fire corridor. Then he sent his attendant ahead to take a look.

"It saved my life," he said.

"I was a Konuan," she said.

"What?"

"I'm just going to check around," Cilreth said.

"Send an attendant," Magnus told Cilreth on his link.

"A Trilisk machine turned me into a Konuan," Telisa continued. "There's another one, a technology-using one. It has a stash of weapons and equipment. Maybe even Trilisk things. I was there in the building with you and that woman."

"Arakaki," he said. His attendant darted into the farthest room ahead, where they had entered under fire. There were blackened spots on the wall where men had been. Only two men remained, untouched but obviously shell-shocked. Magnus judged the entire left side flanking force must have been taken out. Then some remaining missiles must have come into the main room he saw. But they did not get everyone there, so the UED right side flanking force was still intact.

Magnus changed positions. "The threat is from the right now," he said. "Fall back into that room." He indicated the room where Telisa had launched the weapon. "Then we face this direction instead. Their right flank force is untouched, I think."

"Wow, that weapon did a number on the guys," Cilreth said. Magnus saw more evidence of dead UED soldiers through her attendant's feed. His own attendant returned to cover his move to the other room. Meanwhile, a thread of his mind was working though what Telisa had said.

"You were seriously a Konuan? You were put into an alien body, for real?"

And she has a jealous streak for a UED soldier I just met?

"I was trying to save you from the other one, the dangerous one," Telisa said. "But I just got myself shot."

What the...?

"You were there! We killed *you*?"

Now Telisa stole his full attention, though he knew distraction during a battle was foolhardy.

"Then I came back to my original body," she said. "I guess it's a kind of default."

How is that possible? The Trilisks... "You had no link, then? I had no idea. I'm sorry—"

"Of course I don't blame you. Not consciously, anyway," she said with a hint of a smile.

"It's insane. So the dangerous Konuan hunter is still out there."

"Yes. What happened to Arakaki?"

"Once the hunt was over, she took off. I don't know why she didn't capture or kill me. Maybe it was her way of tossing me a favor for helping her kill what we thought was the Konuan that's been hunting them."

"She must have told them about us. Why do they want us dead?"

Magnus thought about the close miss and the lack of heavy hardware being applied in the attack. "Maybe they want to capture us," he said. "They have more than they've used. Unless they're desperately low on munitions."

"Team. Enemy not pursuing." The new message came from Shiny.

"Not pursuing you or me?" Telisa asked.

"However, target of intense interest spotted in ruins," the alien continued. "Prepare to assist with capture of possible Trilisk in lower tunnel system."

Magnus swore. Shiny's announcement was most unexpected, though at this point Magnus stayed focused on the danger. He doubted Telisa would be able to ignore the mention of Trilisks.

"It's good to hear you, Shiny," Telisa said. "We're fighting for our lives, will assist if you get us out of this."

Good call! He pulls us out of the fire; then we help the sucker.

"Battle machine outside neutralized," Shiny reported. "Enemies moving in to flank, trap, surprise you from below."

"Below us? Which direction are you? Should we make a run for it?"

"Proceed south. Will cover retreat, withdrawal, emergence from building."

Chapter 24

Keziph scurried over the landscape rapidly. There were bipeds nearby, running, hiding, or dying. For the moment, Keziph and its broodmates were safe. It crawled into a breach in the rocks and covered under a dense group of native plants. Once safe, Keziph felt less inclined to remain in control.

Keziph prepared to change stances. Deprived of its natural body or a suitable robotic equivalent, the act was no longer effortless. It required a transition delay. And of course, there was no longer any physical component. The body it occupied merely paused for a moment.

Finally Micet came to the fore.

"The test worked perfectly," Micet told its broodmates. "Though hardly more than this Wehhid body, the newcomer species is capable of receiving us. The test subject was successfully transmitted and reset."

Micet considered the other, more complex creature that had assaulted the bipeds. Its hardware was somewhat more advanced, but Micet lacked the preparation. Supersedure into that form was more tempting but carried huge risks. Micet prepared a summary for Cayach and changed stance.

Cayach came to the fore in the slow, troubled way of this body.

For the thousandth time, Cayach felt loss. Loss for its own bodies, loss for its god, and loss for its home to the methane breathers.

Cayach heard one of the clumsy bipeds stomping by within the sensitive Wehhid audial sphere. The biped cursed aloud. And Cayach instantly recognized it. The leader of the original biped explorers.

Cayach decided on a final change of plan. Rather than superseding one of the worshipers who had traveled here to serve it, a superior option stood ready: the leader of the primitive soldier beings. Its status would make the seizure of a starship simple, and would allow for a smoother transition into dominance among any others of their kind. The only problem Cayach saw would be the lack of neural shackles: its followers were free to think and act however they chose, and the recent defeat made them likely to choose desertion over obedience.

"That one. We will use that body to escape."

Micet replied slowly, submerged: "That race can only hold two of us conscious. But those two could be in-stance at once!"

It was a strange compromise. The original Trilisk body allowed all three broodmates to observe and express, though only the in-stance one could control the body, and with such control came temporary dominance. The flat, native creature allowed all three relative equal status, though they retained their accustomed mode of operation: it was second nature to switch stances and operate with one broodmate dominant at any given moment.

The bipeds were another flavor: their minds were split into halves, allowing two in-stance entities at once, a concept half-amusing, half-horrifying to the Trilisk broodmates.

"I leave it to you two, then, to take us to the world of the Holoeum where we can find a new body and a fresh god," Cayach said. "That is our objective. I will submerge until you have brought it to pass."

Micet took control and issued the final commands. The process was almost instantaneous: Micet found himself with Keziph, together in the body of a biped.

"Really this creature is—" Micet stopped as one of its limbs moved, though Micet did not command it to do so. "Ah! So disturbing!"

"I see what you mean," Keziph said. "This could be very bad. If you interfere while I am in combat, our effectiveness will be compromised."

"We are in combat," Micet said. "There are enemies about. We should find our servants and organize them for the journey to Holoeum. Forward, Keziph," it urged. "Destroy any who do not obey."

Then Micet tried to de-stance, though it was not fully successful. Broodmates often sought to remain in-stance, and the idea that someday it would be unable to de-stance had never occurred.

Keziph felt it, too, but did not complain. It tested the biped's arms and legs. Then it puzzled over the communication device it found in its head. It was definitely very different, very not-itself. The primitive race had only recently fused themselves to their machines. The results were less than satisfactory.

The device reported a lower-ranking companion nearby. Keziph found the other biped within the minute. It was covering behind some rocks with a few scavenged backpacks and weapons lying about.

Keziph started to communicate, then realized it didn't have the ability.

"Micet…"

Keziph instinctually tried to change stance, but Micet *was already there*.

Micet supplied the words. Keziph and Micet spoke them together.

"Take what you can. We're headed for the ship," they croaked.

"We've lost, Colonel," the Terran said. "They have an alien on their side. Ships in orbit. And they've destroyed all our hardware planetside."

"We're taking what we have and getting onto the last assault transport."

"No, sir. It's over."

Keziph raised his Terran weapon and shot the demoralized soldier in the head. The Terran fell back, utterly dead.

"What in the hell are you doing? You brought us to this, and now you're killing your own men?" came an urgent communication from another Terran. "You bastard!"

Keziph looked around with the Terran body's binocular vision. The communication device in Keziph's head identified the speaker: Captain Arakaki.

Keziph brought up the host's weapon again.

The creature who had challenged him dove for cover. Keziph opened fire. It was as if the primitive device in Keziph's tiny manipulators had been designed to miss. The projectiles flew almost straight from the barrel. They only angled slightly toward the prey. Once the projectiles had flown past, missing, they did not return to try again.

Keziph tossed the puny weapon away. If only its god could hear it, destroying the attacker would be such a simple thing. But it had been reduced to this.

The creature it had tried to kill was running away. It turned as it ran to point its own simple weapon at him. Keziph grasped a red rock and charged forward.

The Terran's coherent light weapon lanced out. Keziph interposed the rock. The moisture within the obstacle heated rapidly, causing the rock to crack and pop into several pieces. Keziph turned aside to keep the incoming radiation from hitting him cleanly, but the attack was already over. The Terran weapon didn't have enough energy to keep it up.

The Terran turned to run. It couldn't match Keziph's speed.

Suddenly an explosion threw Keziph high into the air. It tucked and spun, riding the shock wave gracefully.

One of its two large legs was leaking red fluid. A shard of metal was buried inside it. Keziph tried out the leg. It still worked for now, though it was weaker and the fluid continued to erupt.

The device in its skull announced medical attention was necessary. It instructed Keziph to staunch the bleeding. The primitive battle suit it wore seemed to sense the danger, and it tightened around the wounded limb.

"Are we dying?" it asked, feeling Micet was still there.

"No. The link says we can block off the wound and continue. Forget that one," Micet suggested. "In fact, forget them all. There may be a few aboard the ship eager to flee with us. The ship is this way."

Michael McCloskey

Chapter 25

Telisa and Magnus sheltered inside a Konuan building to await the outcome of the local battle. Confident in Shiny's superior weapons, Telisa figured it was only a matter of cleanup. She did not want to get dropped by a stray round now after making it through so much. Cilreth had turned on her stealth suit and returned to the *Clacker* with a few new Vovokan battle drones in orbit around her.

"Cilreth may not be cut out for this," Magnus said.

"Are you kidding? She's tough as nails," Telisa said.

"She mumbled something about staying in the ship next time."

"She's just blowing off some steam."

"Could be. She was attacked by a native predator. It left two holes in her suit," Magnus said.

"Is she okay? We shouldn't have let her go by herself."

"It was a close thing, but she's not injured."

Telisa hesitated a moment, then continued. "I have an odd admission to make," she said. "In the interest of full disclosure…I may have had children with someone else while I was a Konuan."

Magnus just stared at her for a moment. "Uhm. Oh."

"It wasn't by choice. I kept dropping these eggs from my tendrily-ventricle-thingies, and I couldn't carry them all for long, so I hid them away. But that other one might have found them and fertilized them. Or something like that. I didn't touch the guy, I promise."

Magnus's eyebrows came up as she spoke. "I knew you were obsessed with aliens, but I didn't expect you to go that far," he said, smiling a bit.

Telisa lifted her hands in a "not my fault" display.

Magnus nodded. "Okay, thanks for letting me know. I think. I, myself, did not fertilize any eggs while you were gone."

She laughed. He smiled as well, showing her he wasn't angry.

Of course he's not. There would be no reason to be. That was just weird.

"And that woman?" she asked.

"Arakaki. She's UED. Or she was. She's good. If she's still alive, we need her."

"What?"

"We could use her. She's tough. A survivor. We could use her on the team."

"You and three women. I see where this is going."

"Don't be insane. She's good. You'd agree if you would quit thinking of her as some kind of competition. Look, we'll recruit two or three men. You can help choose them."

"I suppose you're right," Telisa said. "But the more people we let in, the more we risk fragmentation of purpose. We'll have to be beyond careful in recruiting."

"Yes. Jack was good at it. He chose you. And he knew you were the right person for the job before you even heard the pitch. Thomas was like, oh no, she's going to tell her father and we're all going to get arrested, but you just signed on and never looked back, just like Jack said you would."

"What's Shiny up to now?"

"We can go take a look," Magnus said. "The UED scattered. Shiny says the survivors are headed back to their camp."

"Shiny saves us yet again."

"He seems to be sticking with us. I guess you were probably right about him." Magnus said it with difficulty. Telisa accepted the statement and did not gloat.

"Let's go find our Vovokan benefactor." She stood and checked her suit. Luckily Momma Veer had foreseen camping out on dirty, dusty worlds and provided the skinsuit with a charge-and-repel system for keeping dust from sticking.

"Maybe Veer Industries should run the Earth government."

Magnus shrugged. "Maybe it already does."

Telisa and Magnus moved toward Shiny's position. Their link maps told them the alien worked at the site where Telisa's human body had been in the tube. Before they arrived, they could hear digging machines. The sounds of dirt and rubble being shifted carried far across the ruins.

At least it's not the sounds of gun and rocket fire anymore.

The pair kept sharp. Even though Shiny's orbs patrolled the area, they were afraid of being ambushed by a UED survivor. Telisa also thought again about the predator that had attacked Cilreth, or whatever might have caused the Konuan to make all those grilles. Telisa had one Vovokan attendant orb left, but both of Magnus's were still with him, though she swore one of them wobbled like a bent tire.

The first thing Telisa saw of the destination was a deep pit surrounded by four large digging machines. The machines were built upon multiple legs like the Vovokan walkers. They approached the edge of the dig site. Telisa looked down. The top of the Trilisk chamber had been opened like a living thing, cut across and propped open like a patient's chest in major surgery.

Two machines with long arms and crane-cable claspers loaded another body-switch apparatus into a huge transport vehicle as she watched.

Cilreth appeared nearby.

"Hi. I thought you were hiding in the *Clacker*," Telisa said.

"I guess my curiosity is stronger than my sense," Cilreth said.

"That's true of all of us, or we wouldn't be here," Telisa answered. "These devices are amazing. Though I'm not sure we want to use them. Interesting as it was to become a Konuan, I don't think I'll be switching bodies again anytime soon."

"I don't know if we can sell them, either," Cilreth said.

Telisa opened her mouth to say *of course we can* but then stopped. In the hands of a private client, what damage could be done?

"I can't believe it. You might be right," Telisa said. "Have I become like the world government? Deciding these artifacts are too powerful to be in the hands of a single individual?"

"Just switching to alien bodies doesn't sound like it would be harmful to others. Freedom of physiology has already been granted to individuals wanting to live in regrown or android bodies," Cilreth said.

"This technology highly unbalancing to Terran society," Shiny interrupted.

"How so?" asked Magnus.

"Supersedure target possesses enhanced physiology. Transfer endows subject with artificial gains."

"How do you know? Maybe Konuan are just fast and strong."

"Trilisks enhanced host bodies. Faster, stronger, greater intellectual receiving capacity. Likely increase in longevity of host."

"Wait. By how much are we talking about here?"

"Potentially infinite, limitless, immortal."

Telisa and Magnus just stood thinking it through. Cilreth was the first to respond aloud.

"We can't sell even one," Cilreth said. "They could be adapted to put a person into a fake human body, stronger, faster, and immortal. Wait. *I* need the damn thing!"

Magnus lifted his hand. "Let's not get ahead of ourselves."

"Shiny, how old are you?" Telisa asked.

"Fifty-two Earth years. In anticipation of next question, Vovokan lifespan expected over three hundred Earth years."

Cilreth shifted uncomfortably. "So you mentioned a Trilisk. What if…that Konuan has a Trilisk in it?"

"What?" asked Magnus.

"That would explain so much. Like how there's only one Konuan left. How it killed off so many. How it had worshipers who said it was amazingly wise."

"Agree, assent, concur. Anomalies detected on surface quite probably align with movements of Konuan hunter. Urge priority of capturing it."

"How can we find it? Can you detect it?"

"Possible on planet surface," Shiny said. "More difficult within Trilisk complex."

"Don't we need to take these artifacts and leave?" Cilreth asked.

"Loading machines can complete process," Shiny said. "Trilisk specimen more valuable. Trilisk possess keys to understanding. Be notified: Terran approaches from southeast. No violent intent indicated."

***

"I'm here to see Magnus," she told the sphere. It reacted almost immediately, moving to one side. Another sphere appeared on her left.

I guess I just keep moving forward.

She walked along an ancient street between two old buildings, then into a wide patch of native plants. When she emerged, she caught sight of a couple of the scientists ahead. Large alien-looking machines were working on a dig. A person came forward. Magnus.

"Please don't shoot. I would like to speak in peace," she called out. She waited a moment, then walked forward with her empty hands held before her.

"Oh. It's you," Magnus said.

"Who? Is she Arakaki?" the younger woman said. Her voice held an edge. Arakaki guessed she was Telisa.

"Captain Arakaki, UED. Ex-captain, I guess, considering the state of my unit and United Earth Defiance." She stood straight and extended her hand.

Telisa stared at Magnus, waiting for an explanation. An older woman with silvering hair and dark eyes appeared on her right. Arakaki was surprised she hadn't seen the older one. She berated herself silently, then stepped forward to accept her handshake.

Ah. She's wearing a space force stealth suit.

"I'm Cilreth," she said.

Why didn't she divulge her rank? No reason to let the enemy know, I guess, even a defeated enemy. Or she's been out of the force for a while.

Arakaki nodded stiffly.

"It's probably no use turning yourself in to us," Magnus said. He hesitated. Telisa looked angry, but she wasn't saying anything on any link channel Arakaki could hear.

Those two are having a disagreement over my sudden appearance, Arakaki thought. *I'd love to hear that link channel.*

Arakaki smiled. "Oh? So you were telling the truth about not being space force, then?"

Magnus nodded.

"You're very powerful for an independent," she said. *Organized crime? With an alien on their side, no less.*

"We're after the Konuan. It's a Trilisk," Magnus said.

No way. No way. "Come again?"

"The Konuan we killed was actually Telisa here. She used Trilisk machines to switch bodies. I know.

Impossible. But so is half the other stuff the Trilisks can
do. Anyway, the Konuan that's been hunting us might be a
Trilisk."

Arakaki shifted uncomfortably.

*Perhaps I was knocked unconscious by hallucinogenic
gas?*

***

"So you guys came for these artifacts? What do they
do?"

*She's not sure whether to believe us, so she changed
the subject,* Telisa thought. She wondered if Arakaki
wondered if they were a legal operation.

"We don't know everything about them. At least one
transfers your…consciousness into another creature. In
this case, it put me in a Konuan."

"A simulation."

"No, it was real. You killed me."

Arakaki looked at Telisa carefully.

Is that concern or skepticism?

"Your brain architecture couldn't map directly to—"
Arakaki started.

"I know. I didn't even have the same number of eyes
or legs. I don't know how they did it, but the Trilisks
mastered some kind of adaptive process that allowed me to
stay very much myself, even though I had another body.
The physical control had to have been helped along a great
deal. I was clumsy, confused, but it wasn't like starting
over as a baby in a new body. The transfer mechanism
somehow did a 'best fit' analysis of how my old body
moved and connected it to my new one."

"Trilisk capable of transfer, replacement, supersedure
of sentient creatures to other forms. Natural bodies and
artificial ones known to be within their capabilities," Shiny

said. Arakaki looked around, probably searching for the source of the voice.

That one's going to be a surprise, Telisa thought.

"That's beyond amazing. Think about it. They came here who knows how long ago. They made their support base to answer prayers of sentient beings, and then they transfer into—supersede—the natives."

"Shiny said Trilisks had an outpost on Earth," Magnus pointed out.

Oh my Five Entities.

"They may have become human. They may have...could some of them *still be* human?"

"Too bad for them," Cilreth said sarcastically. "The outpost eventually crapped out on them. They would have been stuck there, without their precious prayer machines, they'd be reduced to...well, Stone Age, or whatever we were at the time."

"We were wondering if some of them stayed human. Their children, if they had any, would be human. I think."

"We don't know if they came to other planets specifically to take over the native bodies. This may have been nothing more than a research project, or even an entertainment to them," Magnus pointed out. "Travel to strange worlds, see new things, try new alien bodies. It could have been a vacation package for all we know."

Arakaki listened to the amazing conversation, left behind. But she appeared intensely interested.

"Well that Trilisk, tourist or not, has killed hundreds of Terrans, maybe more."

"So much for the benevolent Trilisk ideas."

"It may be a single example," Telisa said. "It doesn't represent its race any more than a single human can represent us. Besides, it may have been driven insane by loneliness, or the collapse of its prayer receiver, or who knows. There's so much we don't know."

"Okay, now I know you're unreasonably biased toward anything alien," Cilreth said. "I agree we know nothing for sure, but a growing body of evidence suggests Trilisks may have been nasty characters."

"It might not be a Trilisk. It could be someone else in a special Konuan body just like I was."

"I found a body in one of the tubes when I was searching for you," Cilreth said. "I'm pretty sure it was a Trilisk corpse."

"I need to see it!" Telisa exclaimed.

"Wait," Magnus said. "We have to go after it as soon as possible to have any hope of catching it."

"I got you a sample," Cilreth slipped in. "Including an important piece of what may have been a body-wide link or enhanced nervous system that worked like a distributed link. Hell, I don't know. I got you a sample of some damn thing or other."

"Send Shiny after it," Telisa said. "We'll follow. He can message us with directions. I need to see that body. We need to take this equipment with us. We can't leave. Not even to chase a Trilisk."

"Okay. Besides, it may still not be that particular Trilisk in the body. It could still be some other creature, or another Trilisk…"

"If you're hunting the thing, then I want in," Arakaki said.

"I don't think we need any—" the younger woman started, then stopped. To cover the awkward silence while she argued with Magnus in private, Arakaki offered a bit of a carrot.

"Well, I can offer you a lot in return. For starters, I know where your Trilisk is and what it looks like."

"What? How is that possible?" Cilreth asked.

"Just tell us," Magnus said. "Earn our trust. We aren't ready to offer you anything yet."

"Holtzclaw. Our commander. He just radically changed personalities. Toward the rabidly homicidal. I think the Trilisk just took him over," Arakaki said.

"How do you know your man didn't just cut and run? Losing the battle may have broken him."

"Are you kidding? He hadn't given in to the Earth forces yet. Years after we lost. Do you think he would just leave? He was determined to fight to the bitter end. And bring all of us with him. Even if he was finally giving up, he'd never leave without all of us."

"And what about you? You're giving up all that loyalty just like that?"

"I used to be loyal. Until it dawned on me that we'd lost and we had no hope of ever winning. Once I had accepted that, it was just a matter of biding my time. At least, until we came here and the Konuan started hunting us down."

"We could do a truth check," Cilreth said.

"Not really. Who knows what kind of link she has? The UED may have made modifications to their officers."

Magnus sighed. "We have an option. There's Shiny."

"What about him?" Telisa asked.

"How much you want to bet he can tell if one of us is lying?"

Telisa frowned. "I suppose he might be able to do that."

"I think it's part of why he's still aligned with us. He knows we're not going to switch on him because he can tell we're sincere about working with him."

Arakaki shifted uncomfortably. "Who's Shiny?"

Chapter 26

Kirizzo scanned again for anomalies as his Terran allies attempted to explain odd aspects of his physiology and culture to the newcomer named Arakaki. His allies had accepted her into their group after Kirizzo scanned her statements for deception. She had been truthful in expressing her desire to chase the probable Trilisk. He had not yet made an appearance within her sensory range, and saw no need to as yet. There remained higher priorities.

The assertion that the target had taken Terran form altered his search configuration considerably. The possibility now existed that the target had moved back above ground but evaded his detection grid. Kirizzo produced another signature profile and released it on half his surface monitoring assets.

Drones shot around above the ruins at high speeds to cover ground while using the new profile. Kirizzo almost immediately picked up the target again. The anomalies were indeed centered on a Terran retreating back toward the UED base. Several other Terrans moved with him.

Suddenly his allies became extremely agitated.

"Shiny, what's going on? Are we being attacked? Are you attacking someone?" Telisa transmitted.

"Negative. Scanning for target. Verified Trilisk superseded a Terran."

"You don't hear—oh. I mean, do you sense that atmospheric disturbance?"

Kirizzo looked through his mountains of monitoring data. He did not make progress until he had the key insight: the Terran sense of hearing.

"Speculation, theory, explanation: scout drone's supersonic velocities disturbed local, nearby, proximate gaseous envelope. Please acknowledge: is theory probable, likely, satisfactory?"

"Oh, sonic booms? Yes, it sounds like that. Okay, as long as they're yours. Thanks. So you think it's in a Terran body as Arakaki said?"

"Over 90 percent probability. Otherwise, a Trilisk deception, misdirection, trick."

"Can we capture him?"

"Routing location to you. Move in," Kirizzo urged.

It did not appear he had to offer any incentive in trade. The Terrans gathered their equipment rapidly. They spoke of the target among themselves, including the new one. Kirizzo activated his walking machine and paralleled their course.

"This Trilisk is likely very dangerous," Magnus said.

"Scratch the likely part. It is dangerous," Arakaki added.

"Theorize, suppose, expect target has exhausted advanced resources. Otherwise, UED forces likely, probably, certainly, extinct," Kirizzo said.

As the Terrans moved out toward the suspected Trilisk, Kirizzo monitored the Terrans and the target intently.

Kirizzo detected a statistically significant increase in communications from the Terran named Telisa directed to her mate Magnus. His initial impression was that Telisa reacted with hostility to his interaction with the new female of breeding age. After all, they had encountered other Terrans without eliciting this response from Telisa. Perhaps she attempted to solidify her position with Magnus in anticipation of a possible cooperative shift in Magnus toward the new female. In any case, Telisa was agitated and it appeared to have something to do with the new interloper.

Kirizzo made a note to investigate other differences between this female and the older one called Cilreth, but he assumed it had to do with the superior fertility of the UED soldier. Her suitability as a mate must be an order of magnitude higher than Cilreth; therefore she was more of a threat to Telisa's status. Perhaps Kirizzo would get to observe a shift to competition within the tightly knit Terran group at last.

Updates came in from his many machines on the planet, shifting his attention away from the interplay between the Terrans. Enemies ahead launched projectiles at the walker. At the same time, his Terran allies came under fire. One of Kirizzo's attendant drones serving Magnus reported a projectile intercept, then another.

"Take precautions against enemy action," Kirizzo transmitted.

"Uhm, yes, Shiny," Telisa said. "We hit the dirt. We have a sniper. I think they're far away."

Kirizzo checked Telisa's position. She was indeed on the ground, along with her companions. Kirizzo found it odd how her phraseology had not changed even though the surface was now hard and rocky: "hit the dirt" remained her chosen expression. If Terran terminology was this inflexible, perhaps the Terrans themselves were inherently inflexible. Could this explain their reluctance to switch to competitive mode?

"Light screen of combatants ahead. Probable goal: delay pursuit," Kirizzo summarized for them. He sent along his sensor readings. The closest soldier in the screen was over a kilometer from their position. More rounds came in from the UED Terrans. Though they likely did not have clear targets, their projectiles knew roughly what they were shooting for. Or were they more likely configured for what they were *not* shooting for? At least in the case of the other Terrans it was likely they would be targets of opportunity for passing rounds.

"It'll take awhile to advance against them," Magnus said.

"A soluble problem," Kirizzo said.

"What are you doing?"

"Launching countermeasures," Kirizzo said. He allocated drones to four small positions held by pairs of Terrans ahead of them. His allies talked more among themselves. Kirizzo allocated more attendant spheres to them so that each of them would have at least two protectors.

The four sniper nests exploded in quick succession.

"Threat neutralized. May continue at current, present, existing pace."

Once again a stir went through the Terrans working with him.

"I knew those men. You didn't have to kill them," Arakaki said on the group channel.

"Terrans seek to delay pursuit," Kirizzo informed them. "Target moving away."

"She means those soldiers are not against us," Telisa explained to him. "They are not in competition with us; they don't understand their leader has been taken over by an alien."

"What exactly are these things flying around us?" Arakaki asked.

"Don't kill any other Terrans please," Telisa said to Kirizzo. "They are not our enemies."

"May further delay pursuit. Offer in exchange 5 percent more resource allocation from industrial seed. Alternative, secondary, additional offer: increased access to Vovokan military hardware."

"What?"

"Is he offering us things in exchange for our buy-in on killing more of my fellow UED soldiers?" Arakaki asked. Her voice indicated higher than average levels of strain or emotional disturbance.

"We can't bargain with you on this, Shiny," Telisa said.

"Seven percent more resource allocation from—"

"We can't bargain with human lives," Arakaki said.

Perhaps an individual's worth to society had to be fully measured before the Terrans would allow exchange of the individual's life for resources. Kirizzo changed tack.

"Offering 1.3 times Terran average life valuation on Earth in any currency or resource for license, permission, agreement to kill intervening Terrans without breaking existing alliance," he offered.

"We refuse!" Arakaki said.

"Wait a minute," Magnus said. He sent further private communications among the other Terrans. Kirizzo did not intercept the signals, though he might well have done so if things were less hectic. The Terrans were obviously hung up on a point perhaps practical but more likely terminology oriented. Perhaps the one called Magnus could see a way through this particular intercultural maze. Kirizzo wasn't sure what the conflict was, but he hoped Magnus could mesh their negotiation styles quickly.

"Don't kill them unless any of us are in real danger," Cilreth suggested.

"Goal in danger, wish to prevent escape of valuable target," Kirizzo said.

"Where is the target going to go? You're tracking it, right? We don't need to kill these people," Telisa said.

"Target may descend into Trilisk tunnels to escape detection. May escape in UED space vessel."

"He wouldn't get past the *Thumper*, though?

"Unlikely, improbable, doubtful."

Kirizzo entered a planning phase. What should he do if the Terrans remained obstructionistic to the capture of the Trilisk in a Terran shell? Proceed without their assistance. Take the Trilisk back to the base in his own ship. The *Clacker* would be left with the valuable Trilisk artifacts, but he would have a Trilisk. The trade would be in his favor. Should he relocate the base in that case to avoid further Terran entanglement? It would depend on what he could learn from the Trilisk. Would it be dangerous to allow the Trilisk close to the AI? It was a troubling thought he hadn't considered. A Trilisk might well be able to undo his handiwork with the prayer blocker and simply run rampant with it. Then Kirizzo would be the captured specimen. A great deal of time would be required to complete the phase. He would be better served by switching back to action now.

The intervening Terrans had all expired. Kirizzo's countermeasures had been more effective than he had expected. He decided to soften the blow to his allies upon reporting the result.

"The Terrans ahead have scattered," he said. "Some casualties among them. Target now within confines of UED encampment."

"Do they have any defenses?" Magnus asked. Kirizzo prepared an analysis to reply, but Arakaki responded.

"Mostly the Guardians were the defense. I understand many of them have been destroyed?"

"Affirmative, correct, verified."

"They may have some grenades set. I could probably make it in myself, and they wouldn't target me."

"What would you do by yourself?"

"Kill the damn thing, of course," Arakaki said. "Your alien friend isn't hesitating to kill any of them. Let me in there and take a crack at it. Maybe I can save the rest. If you all go in, then there will be more deaths."

"No personnel left in camp," Kirizzo told them. "Survivors gathering at grounded assault ship."

"Then we all go in," Magnus said. "Arakaki's on point. She'll let us know if any friendly grenades are armed within range."

"Unless Holtzclaw—the Trilisk, that is—reset some grenades and locked me out. I encountered him, or it, whatever, just after he shot one of our own. He knows I'm alive."

"Did he have time?" asked Telisa.

"Who knows what that thing is capable of," Cilreth said.

"Sending more drones," Kirizzo said. He routed more nearby machines toward the Terrans. "Within their capability to intercept Terran grenades. Two per host provides over 80 percent success rate outside the blast radius. Sending one ahead to seek active grenades."

"Handy," Arakaki said. Her voice feigned a trivial assessment belied by her physiological readings. The Terran Arakaki was, in fact, in a high state of stress. He intensified his study. Could this Terran have been altered by the Trilisk? He found no evidence to support the idea. A simpler explanation was simply that her life was under threat. Though as a trained soldier, she should be calm. He compared her readings to those of Magnus. They were comparable, so he dropped the line of investigation.

The anomalous readings changed subtly. They were centered on a Terran starship set slightly into a hillside.

"Target most likely entered vessel on far side of encampment."

The ship's power systems spiked. The primitive Terran gravity spinner was being powered up. Meanwhile, his allies had reached the edge of the obfuscation device that covered the UED encampment.

"Forget it. Get back!" Arakaki transmitted. "He's starting up the engines."

Kirizzo considered the countermeasures at his disposal. Though the walker commanded sufficient firepower to bring down the Terran assault ship with precise strikes, destroying the Terran vessel seemed inadvisable. He could well kill the Terran body Holtzclaw inside, even though it enjoyed superhuman status.

Instead, Kirizzo contacted his starship in orbit and instructed it to prepare to intercept the Terran assault ship.

His own Terran allies ran to safety. There was a brief discussion about taking shelter in the cavern entrances just inside the camp, but the threat of traps instead sent the Terrans moving alongside the perimeter and toward a large fissure. Should he inform the Terrans that the more massive Chigran Callnir Four predators preferred to lair in the largest fissures? No. The group was well armed and could likely survive any such encounter.

The Terran ship lifted from the surface. It did not attempt to use its ground attack munitions or its propellant drive to attack as his allies feared. Instead it proceeded optimally toward orbit.

"Shifting attention away from the surface. Obtain items of interest."

"Will do, Shiny, good luck," Telisa responded.

The anomalous readings continued, centered on the Terran ship. Either the Trilisk truly was aboard or it had sophisticated means of tricking Kirizzo. The Gorgalan wondered if the Trilisk was aware a non-Terran hunted it. Perhaps it thought it only needed to escape any Terran forces in orbit.

The *Thumper* released independent probes and weapons to form a screen that would follow and intercept the fleeing ship. But the Terran vessel was slow and clumsy. It was easily intercepted by the *Thumper* itself, despite the huge mass difference.

Something changed. The odd readings Kirizzo used to track the alien disappeared. He switched away from its Terran body signature. Nothing. He switched back to the original parameters he had used to scan the planet. Still nothing. More scans on the surface at the lift off site did not reveal the Trilisk, either.

The *Thumper* moved in and hacked the Terran vessel's control systems to shut down its gravity spinner. The ship was in his grasp. Several of his remote probes and pieces of ordnance attached themselves to its surface.

"I have captured the UED vessel," he reported to the Terrans. "However, no Trilisk signature detected aboard vessel. Anomalies have disappeared, ceased, vanished."

"What? He's still down here somewhere?"

"Unknown, uncertain, unascertained."

The first possibility was that the retreat to the Terran vessel had been a ruse. The second possibility was that the Trilisk was still in the ship but could not be detected. A third possibility was that the Trilisk had rendezvoused with an undetectable ship, boarded it, and left.

Kirizzo tried to think of other explanations. After a moment, another theory surfaced: Trilisks might be so advanced, they might not need starships to travel between the stars. But if so, why the ruse? Perhaps the method required distance from the planet to achieve. There was no way of knowing. Better to concentrate on conventional explanations first? But the target was thought to be a Trilisk. Conventional could hardly describe Trilisks.

"Advise continue search on surface and in orbit," he transmitted to the Terrans. "However, chances of recovering target rapidly diminishing."

The Terrans commandeered two remaining sensor modules from the UED force and started searching for the Trilisk in the body of Holtzclaw. Their search signature lacked sophistication; however, if the Trilisk was still in Holtzclaw, they might succeed.

Kirizzo thought about the sequence of events. Had the moment of transition to the Terran vessel been a ruse? Perhaps it had entered a Trilisk tunnel beneath at that time. But the nearest tunnel went under the west side of the UED camp, where they had been digging for Trilisk technology. He spotted a likely error: the assumption that the Trilisk had none of its own devices to use. Its industrial seed may have been exhausted, broken, or even destroyed in an enemy attack (the methane breathers?), but that did not mean the Trilisk did not have any of its other tools left to use. Perhaps it had been rationing what it had left for dire circumstances.

Kirizzo conducted a search of his own vessel. What if the Trilisk had gotten on board? Kirizzo realized the creature would be very dangerous if it still had functioning devices to use. The Trilisks had been capable of almost anything. How could Kirizzo hope to capture it unless it was deprived of its own technology?

"Trilisk no longer detectable," Kirizzo admitted. "Further analysis required to determine its location."

He did not say he doubted he would ever be able to find it.

"Then what are we going to do?" asked Telisa.

"Recommend return to base for study of Trilisk materials," Kirizzo said. "Many large artifacts available to examine."

"Yes, let's head back. And pray us up some scout replacements," Magnus said.

"And an army of combat robots this time," Cilreth interjected. "And a bunch of high-tech traps."

The new Terran looked perplexed. "What about the hunt?"

"If Shiny doesn't know where it is, then we don't either," Telisa said. "But we can keep looking, and the next best thing is to figure out its toys."

"What kind of a base is this?" Arakaki asked.

Magnus smiled and told her, "You're going to love it."

But the Terran called Telisa did not look at all happy about it.

Chapter 27

"I'm going to check out the *Clacker*'s new course, see what I can learn from the ship," Cilreth said happily. The Terran part of the team had returned to *Clacker* while Shiny ascended to orbit to reunite with his ship Telisa had named *Thumper*.

"Aren't you annoyed that the Trilisk got away?" Telisa asked. She felt a bit more comfortable since Arakaki had retired to a lavish room they gave her half an hour ago. She trusted Magnus's assessment, but it would take time for her to build up her own trust of a stranger.

"Nothing wrong with me my new superhuman body isn't going to fix right up!" Cilreth said brightly.

"Are we really going to do that? I mean…"

"Why not? We live on the frontier; there's no enforcement of any kind out here. And even by UNSF rules, we have the right to alter our own physiology. Look, a couple more decades and you're going to be singing my song, lady," Cilreth said with a bit of an edge.

"Something tells me if the UNSF knew that right was about to include immortal superhuman bodies, they would restrict it," Telisa said. Even as she said it, she felt the old anger again: how dare they dictate to everyone how to live. She had just convinced herself wrong with her own argument.

"All the more reason to resist them, to fight their rules," Cilreth said.

I guess I agree; it's my choice. But the question is, what if everyone got that choice? What would the repercussions be?

"I say go for it," Magnus chimed in. "You'll have forever to think over the ethical consequences of your act." He smiled.

"Guys, we have a major problem! Shiny's ship just blew up!" Cilreth reported.

"What!?" Telisa sent back.

"His ship exploded."

The Trilisk must have done something.

She traded astonished looks with Magnus. Before they could think through how bad the news was, Cilreth delivered an update.

"Shiny's not dead! He's coming to the *Clacker* on a small ship. I have no idea what's up. I'm sending you a pointer to the bay he's headed for. Maybe go meet him in person?"

"Okay," Telisa said. "We'll meet him and hope he's not a Trilisk."

"Weapons!" Magnus snapped. Telisa checked hers. His rifle was out.

Telisa and Magnus ran through the Terranized sections of the *Clacker*. The ship was so large it still had areas for Vovokans, with natural-looking interiors and a sandy floor.

They arrived at a massive airlock with a large circular iris door. The arriving ship wasn't mated with the *Clacker* yet, but Telisa saw she could connect to Shiny.

"What's going on, Shiny?" Telisa transmitted.

"Joining *Clacker*," the buzzing voice replied. "Bringing UED personnel. Did not apprise them of nature of vessel or host."

"What happened to the *Thumper*, I mean?"

"Destroyed ship to increase chances Trilisk neutralized."

Arakaki walked up behind Telisa and Magnus. When she saw their weapons, she drew her laser.

"What are you doing here?" Magnus said out loud.

"Cilreth told me the other UED survivors from the ship may have blown up."

"They should be here in a few minutes," Magnus said. "As far as I know they're all coming. Maybe you can help get them settled in. I don't think they've met Shiny, but I get the feeling you are about to."

Arakaki nodded.

"Shiny says he destroyed his ship hoping to destroy the Trilisk!" Telisa said. "I don't believe it. Does that make sense to you?"

"Not really," Magnus said.

"That's a pretty extreme step," Arakaki said. "It may have worked, though. Suppose the Trilisk has the equivalent of a stealth suit. It may have been anywhere. And it's sharp. Advanced. It could accomplish anything given time."

"So he pulls a fast escape and blows his own ship up to kill it. All on a hunch?" Telisa said.

"To Shiny, that ship is expendable," Magnus thought out loud. "I guess I could see him sacrificing it if he thought there was a 10 percent chance he'd catch the Trilisk by surprise."

"I thought we were going to capture it," Arakaki said. "Not that I'm complaining. I hope the damn thing blew up."

No one fielded any more theories before the ship connected to *Clacker*. The Vovokan airlocks were huge and circular. The iris before them opened soon after the arrival of the *Thumper*'s escape vessel.

Shiny emerged, pattering in on dozens of legs. Arakaki visibly recoiled.

"Damn. That thing makes Cthulhu look cuddly!" Arakaki exclaimed. Her laser pistol hand wavered, but she didn't point it at Shiny. "Uh, no offense," she added.

"It's Shiny, of course," Telisa said. "You get used to it."

"Right." Arakaki didn't sound any happier.

"You could have checked with us. That was…unexpected," Telisa said to Shiny.

"Unexpected, surprise, unpredictable action intended as strategy to catch Trilisk unprepared," Shiny said. "Intend, attempt, hope the extreme maneuver succeeded."

"Succeeded in killing what we hunted?" Arakaki said.

"Trilisk disappearance requires, needs, depends upon advanced means. Trilisk with advanced means more dangerous, deadly, capable."

Arakaki nodded. "It may have been toying with us all along."

"For what reason? Sadistic pleasure?" asked Telisa.

Arakaki shrugged. "It's an alien. I have no idea. But it liked to hunt us."

Let's hope it isn't one of us, Telisa said to Magnus on a private channel.

Shiny will detect it if that's happened.

What if he already has but hasn't said anything? Keeping his hand secret.

You can invent horrible scenarios like that all day long if you want. I haven't slept in forever.

Right.

***

Telisa and Magnus retired to the opulent lodgings of the Clacker while Arakaki ushered in a small group of UED survivors. After a long sleep and an hour of fooling around to make up for lack of intimate opportunities on the job, they lay together in a huge sleep web.

"What are we going to do about the UED guys?" Telisa asked.

"We can drop them off on the frontier, at a small outpost or something."

"We should recruit from among them."

"Probably," Magnus said.

"I'm surprised you don't sound enthusiastic. The others must not be as cute as Arakaki."

"The others are used to being in a unit. One that went through a lot. Their loyalty to each other will be stronger than any loyalty they could feel to Parker Interstellar

Travels. If we hire them, they'll have to be on their own ship or part of some other team."

I wonder if he feels they must hate him for being ex UNSF.

"You're right," she said. "They'll stay tight with each other, and if we found more valuable stuff they would always be tempted to strike off on their own. They might even leave us stranded on a planet somewhere. But what about Arakaki?"

"She's had enough of it. Ready to move on."

He sure knows a lot about her already.

"What if the Trilisk is in one of them?" Telisa asked. *Or one of us.* She knew he had dismissed the idea earlier, but it kept creeping back up on her.

"Shiny doesn't think so."

"He doesn't know. He admits not knowing what happened to the Trilisk. Destroying his own ship was a move of desperation, I think. He could be the Trilisk."

"Maybe. There's not much we can do to prepare for that possibility. There's another aspect of the UED folks we should consider, though. They must hate the Earth government," he said.

"That helps, since we're basically criminals to the UNSF."

"Yes. That could make this work. They can be the frontier part of the PIT team. But they could also be a part of something larger."

"What does that mean?" she asked.

"I mean if you don't like the UNSF then this is your chance to do something about it. Build an organization to replace them. With alien technology and superhuman immortals on your side, you'd have a shot at bringing them down."

"Five Entities, I suppose you're right. I never got into this for war, though, just for the artifacts."

"Accomplishing it without bloodshed would probably be an unrealistic goal. But it wouldn't have to be like the last war. We might be able to pull off a coup. For instance, maybe we could put ourselves into the bodies of the Earth government leaders, then stand down."

Telisa opened her mouth in astonishment. Such an application hadn't even crossed her mind.

"What if we cause an ongoing conflict? What if aliens do attack while things are confused at home?"

Magnus nodded. "Those are both real risks we would face."

I don't even know what I want anymore.

"We need time to think about this," she said.

Michael McCloskey

Made in the USA
Middletown, DE
01 June 2021